PASSPORT TO HAPPINESS

DEBBIE WHITE

CHAPTER 1

*I*t was 1968, and an earth-shattering year for the country. The awful news of Martin Luther King Jr.'s assassination riveted the country, and the citizens mourned the loss of the greatest civil rights leader the world had ever known. Other happenings in the world that were not as momentous included The Beatles exploding onto the music scene with their first hit, "Hey Jude", McDonald's introducing the Big Mac for forty-nine cents, and my turning twelve years old. I was mature for my age—or at least, that is what Momma told me, not with so many words, but with her actions.

It was evident to me at an early age that we didn't have much money. Momma did the best she could with the little we had. We had one television, one phone in the house, and one old gas-guzzling car sitting out in the gravel driveway. It seemed we were a household of one regarding many things, except for Momma and me.

During the summer months, she grew vegetables, and in the fall, she canned them. She learned a hundred different ways to use stewed tomatoes. I decided early on I didn't like tomatoes. That's what happens when you eat something too often, unless it's ice cream or candy. No one ever gets tired of sweets. We may not have had it easy, but we had a roof over our head, clean clothes, and water to bathe.

Oh, and we had love, too. Momma said we didn't need anything else. I guess she had a point.

Momma didn't really talk about Daddy much. She said she loved him, but that he was a wanderer, a free spirit type. She didn't believe in holding him down or holding him back, and well, I guess he chose the road instead of me and Momma. It was okay, though, Momma was more than enough for me. I was an easygoing child with few desires, and I felt Momma met all my needs.

I must have acquired my looks from my wandering dad. I had wavy blonde hair, and the nickname the kids gave me at school was because of my strange amber-colored eyes. Therefore, the nickname *Owl* stuck with me throughout high school. At first, I was self-conscious of this new name, but after I read a book about owls, and discovered how majestic they really were, I rather liked being associated with them. I wore my hair parted down the middle, and on most days, I'd wear it in a ponytail. That part I must have gotten from Momma. She, too, wore her hair in a ponytail.

I guess looking back, some would say Momma was a plain-Jane. I mostly remember her soft, rounded hips, and callused hands—oh, and her ponytail. She spoke softly and was a woman of few words, but the strength she exhibited daily served to make me stronger, as well. She didn't have it easy. Sometimes I'd get angry at my wandering dad, but Momma never said a harmful word about him. I secretly hoped he'd come back, and I think Momma did, too.

In the springtime, we'd have torrential downpours with thunder and lightning, and the occasional tornado. Our house didn't have a basement so when the siren sounded, letting us know one was nearby, we got in the car and drove the three miles to the school. There in the gymnasium, all the families without basements gathered for what turned out to be a very long night for our parents, but a big slumber party for the children.

Summers were hot and humid and our house didn't have air-conditioning. To stay cool, we sat out on the front porch in our underclothes in the dark, waiting for it to be cool enough so we could sleep. We were entertained by watching the fireflies and June bugs flopping all over the place.

Our winters were cold, too, with ice and snow. Weather in West Texas was extreme. I guess you'd say I was used to it.

Our town was very small. Most people lived on ranches with acreage, so having a next-door neighbor was rare. Our closest was my uncle, who actually shared the parcel with us, but he was down the hill and you couldn't actually see his house from ours. I didn't really like him all that much. He hardly spoke, grunting and grumbling mostly, and I tried my hardest to stay as far away from him as possible. However, he was Momma's younger brother and the only living relative we had. I personally felt we would've been better off without him. His front teeth were missing, and he smelled like whiskey all the time. When Momma made me go stay with him for a short time, I hated it. I begged and pleaded with her not to make me go. You'd think she would've understood that something was making me uneasy about him. Parents are sometimes the last to know, and the first not to believe it.

I was thankful for my best friend, Lauren. Without her, my life would've been crap. She rode her bike to my house and we'd sit for hours on the front porch or under the big oak tree and dream of the day we'd leave this old town. She knew how much I hated my uncle, but she pinky promised she wouldn't tell anyone. Lauren still keeps my secret today.

One of our favorite places to visit was the library. We were regulars, and as soon as we walked in, the librarian would smile, and nodding her head, she'd welcome the both of us into her sanctuary. That's what we thought of it anyway. There we could wander through the rows and stacks of books, looking for the one that would take us far away, forgetting about crazy uncles, or boring little towns. I'd find a comfy chair and look at all the glossy pictures of beautiful places in the world—of castles, beautiful lakes and rivers, and hills and valleys that were dotted with wildflowers. We read about customs in faraway places, countries, and cities whose names we couldn't even pronounce, yet were mesmerized by the wonders of the world.

Lauren and I played a game. We had to guess which country we were traveling to by describing the local customs, food, and dress. It's harder than you think. Some of the countries have similar foods and customs. Reading about other places beyond our little piece of the world gave us hope and ambition, and we yearned for the day we would travel to these mysterious places.

If we weren't checking out books from the local library, we were riding our bikes. Besides books, my bike was the next best thing for escaping my humdrum life. Lauren and I'd take off on our bikes and ride the dusty dirt roads that led down to the creek where the cows and other livestock cooled off on hot, humid summer days. We would get off our bikes and throw stones into the water, sometimes startling them. We didn't mean any harm. We loved those big old cows with the warm butterscotch-colored eyes. We would find a grassy area to sit and watch them drink water from the creek while continually swatting the flies off their rear ends with their tails. We'd walk the well-beaten paths along the stream beds and look for wild licorice. It was a summer treat that we indulged in on many an afternoon. I have fond memories of our lazy summer days.

My pre-teen years were typical of any other young girl's, except for my uncle. I vowed that he didn't really exist, and I didn't have the heart to tell my mother what a scumbag he really was. I kept telling myself he was just overly affectionate, and that if he tried going any further, I'd tell. I was only fooling myself, though. He was just waiting. He was waiting until I was older. Thank God, I left home soon after graduation. Who knows what he had in store for me. I wondered how my momma could be such a kind, loving person and have such a dreadful brother. One of the mysteries of life, I suppose.

Most days were the same for me. Get up early, wash up, eat breakfast, and head to school. I loved school; it was another avenue for me to escape. My teachers were fabulous, and they encouraged me to think big. The library was one of my favorite places and between the school library and the one in town, I always had something checked out.

I was becoming a young woman, and Momma explained to me

about the birds and the bees. I wasn't really interested in all of that, but I listened. We had a class on it, too, so some of the things she said rang true with the movie I saw and the textbook I read. I knew that it was even more important that I keep my distance from my uncle. I had overheard my classmates talking about male and female reproductive organs and babies, and well, I didn't want any part of that. I was actually becoming more vocal to Momma about not staying with my uncle alone. I told her I was big enough that I didn't need a babysitter.

"Momma, I can stay home alone for a few hours by myself," I said, standing my ground.

"Okay, baby. Let's give it a try," Momma said looking at me with the saddest eyes I had seen besides the eyes of the cows Lauren and I'd see down at the creek.

And, from that day forward, my uncle only came around when Momma invited him over for supper. I'd sit at the table and be cordial, but I never let him get close to me again after that. I felt free, liberated, and strong. I knew that nothing would stand in my way for happiness ever again.

In 1972, I turned sixteen. I was so excited for a couple of reasons. I was closer to graduating, and I started noticing boys. I guess I'd noticed them before, but I wasn't really interested. Josh turned my head, though, and soon I'd be spending more time with Josh than Lauren. Lauren was upset at first. Thinking back, if it had been the other way around, I'd have been upset, too. At first, we tried to include her, but soon she felt like a fifth wheel and stopped coming around as much. I missed seeing her, but Josh was one of the cutest boys in our school, and his dimples alone were enough to pull me in. His energy and enthusiasm for life are what really got me hooked.

He had big ideas about life beyond Texas, and I found myself drawn right in. He'd come over to my house most evenings and we'd study, or at least that is what I told Momma we were doing. However, we did anything but study during that hour visit. Our focus was to get the heck out of West Texas. He couldn't wait to escape the boredom that this sleepy little town brought, and I shared with him my desire to travel the world. Josh was a smart guy, another attribute I found appealing. He confided in me that he had been checking out a program that offered pay, travel, and education benefits. I was very intrigued by this idea and asked him to tell me more.

"There are opportunities for Foreign Service Specialists," he said.

"Go on, tell me more," I teased.

Josh explained about the State Department's career opportunities for professionals in places like the ones I wanted to visit. I couldn't believe my ears. I asked him how he'd heard about this opportunity.

"At school," he replied. He said he overheard the kids who would be graduating talking about it. I finally had a plan. I was going to finish school and then I was going to apply to this program. I made it a priority to look up the information at the library.

Josh and I spent many an afternoon dreaming about a time when we would flee this godforsaken place. Little did we know that although we had the same career goals, they would take us down different paths, leaving us only the memories of the long, hazy summers sitting under the old oak tree.

During the fall of my senior year, a group of people came to discuss job opportunities. I was hoping that the career fair would bring the people Josh had told me about. I walked up and down, looking at the various tables, reading flyers displayed as I searched for the one that interested me. Finally, I came across a table that said Careers in the Federal Government. I casually looked at the flyers on the table and saw one that said, "Travel to Posts Overseas, in Washington, D.C., and elsewhere in the United States." I picked it up so I could read it again.

I guess I caught the attention of the people sitting at the table because a few seconds after I approached them, the young woman asked me a question. "Are you graduating this year?"

I nodded my head yes.

"Have you ever thought of serving your country in a civilian capacity, and travel to exotic places, earn a decent salary, and have educational opportunities as well?"

I was thinking, but didn't say it, *Are you kidding? That's all I've been thinking about for the last three years.*

Instead, I just said, "Really, how would I do all of that?"

They explained to me that I'd have to fill out an application, apply for a passport, and take a test. I gathered all the information I could, took one of their business cards, and ran like the devil to look for Josh.

That afternoon, I showed Momma the brochures and all the literature the man and woman gave me. She looked it over, then laid it down on the table, and silently walked back to the sink to finish washing off the strawberries from our garden. Momma made the best strawberry shortcake. It was one of my favorites. Living off the land had advantages, and homegrown fruits and vegetables were one of them—as long as you didn't have to eat too much of them—like tomatoes.

"Momma, what do you think about this program?" She didn't utter a word. "The woman at the career fair told me there are educational benefits, too," I added cheerfully, hoping higher education would be the plus that put her in favor of it. Nothing—not a word escaped from her lips. She just stood at the sink washing and slicing strawberries.

"Josh is interested, too. We might be able to travel to some of these places together," I added.

Finally, Momma turned around, and she looked me squarely in the eyes. "Josh?"

I nodded my head.

"Well then, that might not be so bad," she said, as she turned back around to her chore of slicing strawberries.

I got up from the table, took my brochures with me, and went to my bedroom. I lay on my bed looking up at the ceiling, wondering what I could do to convince Momma that it was a great opportunity. I got up and opened my bedroom window to let the air in. At least there was a breeze, although it was warm. A few minutes later I heard my name.

"Jessica, hey, Jessica, it's me, Josh." I looked up to see Josh peering at me with his green eyes through the screen of my window.

"What are you doing?" I asked him, smiling.

"Did you talk to the people about the Foreign Service?"

"Yes, I did. My momma wasn't that impressed."

Josh frowned. "Well, you don't need her permission. You're eighteen now. All you need is your diploma," he said encouragingly.

I jumped up from my bed and ran over to the window. "This is fantastic, Josh!" I said with as much enthusiasm as I could muster.

GRADUATION DAY WAS exciting for the three of us. Lauren was going to go on to college. Josh and I were going to travel the world. Our class was small, and when they called my name to get my diploma, Momma and my uncle clapped loudly and cheered.

Josh's folks were sitting nearby. Josh's family was different from mine. He had a mom and dad, and an older sister. I was a little envious of his situation but learned that it wasn't always greener on the other side. Josh had shared with me that his parents fought a great deal. They drank a lot, too. He wanted to get out of Dodge, as he'd put it. I wanted to get out of Dodge with him.

Like most graduating seniors, Josh and I decided to stay out late. We invited Lauren, too. There wasn't much to do in our sleepy little town, but we decided to make the best of it. Several of our classmates decided to meet at the A&W. We ordered hamburgers, fries, and the thickest shakes you ever saw.

Several of the kids were staying in the area and finding jobs, some were going off to college, and a couple of the guys were joining the military. Secretly, I thought Josh's and my plan was the best and most exciting.

We sat at the tables, ate our food, and sipped our shakes until a worker approached us and said he was closing up shop. Our little group started breaking up, some leaving alone, others traveling with a buddy, and then finally it was just the three of us. I knew this wasn't goodbye for Lauren and me, but it was one step closer, and as I told her I'd see her around, I felt a lump forming in my throat.

"We still have a couple of weeks before we leave. Let's get together before that, okay?"

Nodding her head, she added, "I have some family I have to visit before I take off for college. But I should have at least a day or so to hang out."

I nodded that I understood and the three of us took off down the side of the road that would eventually branch off to our houses. Josh kicked some rocks as we walked and talked about general stuff. I stopped and picked a few wildflowers that were growing along the road for Momma. After a few minutes, we got to the fork in the road.

"See you soon, Lauren," I said as she veered down the street that would take her home.

Josh and I watched as she walked away from us. A tear puddled on my lower lid. It finally found its way out and trickled down my cheek. I reached up and quickly wiped it away.

"You're going to miss Lauren, aren't you?"

"Yes. We've been friends for a long time," I said, reaching out my hand to clasp his.

We walked the next few minutes in silence, neither one of us knowing exactly what we were feeling, or what we wanted to say. We were just happy to be finished with school. We knew we'd be going to Washington, D.C. for training; we just didn't know all the details.

Josh and I spent most of the daylight hours together, and in between seeing him, I'd squeeze Lauren in. I was happy for her—she was going to some big fancy college in Oklahoma.

"I bet you knock the socks off all those big-city boys, Lauren!" I joked with her.

She teasingly smacked me on the shoulder. "I do not want any boyfriends. They're trouble!"

"That's what I thought, too, Lauren, but Josh is different than a lot of the dumb boys we knew in high school. You'll see. You'll find someone who treats you good and makes you happy. Just make sure you keep your grades up, or your daddy will drive up there and snatch you back home!"

We hugged and laughed out loud. Saying goodbye was hard, but growing up was hard and this was part of life. We vowed we would keep in touch, but as time drifted on and I traveled abroad, it became increasingly harder to keep that promise.

CHAPTER 2

The big black sedan drove up in front of our house. My palms were sweaty, and my heart was racing a mile a minute. Momma was as calm as a cucumber. A man in a dark business suit came strolling up the walk toward our front door. He knocked twice.

"Momma, he's here. The driver is here," I squealed.

I'll never forget as long as I live the forlorn look on Momma's face as we were driving away. She casually waved until she couldn't see the car anymore. I can only imagine what she did afterward. She probably went back inside and shed a few tears.

The driver took Josh and me to the airport. Neither one of us had ever flown before. I was excited, but at the same time, my nerves were getting the best of me. Fortunately for us, we cut our teeth on a short flight, which prepared us for what we would later deem as red-eye flights from hell.

We flew into Dulles, where our team leader picked us up. Agent Perry, as she identified herself, was a lovely woman. She was about five foot eight, slim, with light brown hair and hazel eyes. She wore her hair in a clip high up on her head. She was dressed in black slacks and a buttoned-down white blouse with a black blazer. She had a very stern look about her, but I'd later discover it was just for show. On the inside, she was warm as apple pie just out of the oven. We drove in silence to the dormitories that would become our home for the next couple of weeks. Although it was 1974, coed dorms were considered liberal even by big-city standards, so there was one for the men and one for the women. The coed dining facility was located on the lower level of the women's dormitory.

Agent Perry said for us to get a good night's sleep, as the next couple of weeks would involve studying and physical strength training as well as learning firearms proficiency. Josh and I looked at each other. "Shoot a gun?" I asked.

Agent Perry confirmed what we had heard. "Our consulates are in some very dangerous places. You must be prepared to defend yourself," she said as she'd rehearsed for every group of trainees that came through the doors.

Josh and I weren't sure if we should show any affection toward one another, so we bid each other good night and vowed to see each other at breakfast. He went toward the male dorm and I went to the other. I walked up the stairs to the second floor and down the long hallway, looking for my room. I stopped in front of the door that said 222. I was excited, but also a little nervous. I knew we'd have roommates. I wasn't sure if she was already settled in, or if I'd be first in the room. I started to put my key in the door but decided to give it a jiggle, and sure enough, it was unlocked. I slowly turned the knob and opened the door.

I entered the room, and on the bed near the window sat a black girl. Later, I'd hear others describe her as "light-skinned." It didn't matter to me if she was light-skinned, dark-skinned, or some other variation of *skin*.

It was true—I didn't have much experience with black people. Our town had a separate area where they lived and even had a different school for the black kids. Only during harvest time did the two races mix. Momma would trade her tomatoes for Mr. Henry's okra, and Ms. Violet would trade her collard greens for Momma's snap peas. It was funny. They'd talk, and laugh it up like they were old friends.

Then Momma and I'd walk back to our house with a word never spoken about it again until the next harvest.

Once I started high school, we had a couple of black kids transfer in from other places. Although I was always cordial to them, they pretty much stuck together. They walked to classes, ate their lunch, and walked home together. I guess that's just the way things are in a small town, or perhaps it was just the way of the times. I guess you could say I was happy when I opened the door to room 222.

I walked in and shut the door behind me. Seeing that she was already sitting on a bed near the window, I figured she'd already claimed her side of the room.

"Hi, my name is Jessica McCarthy," I said.

"Hi, my name is Roberta Robinson, but my friends call me Birdie."

"Birdie ... That's a cool name. I don't tell many people this, but my friends call me Owl!"

"Birdie and Owl, roommates," we both said laughing.

"May I call you Birdie?"

She nodded her head yes. "Do you want me to call you Owl, or Jessica?"

I thought about it for a second. "I'm trying to leave the past in the past. Please call me Jessica."

Looking a little surprised, but honoring my wish, she reached out and shook my hand. "It's nice to make your acquaintance, Jessica."

We were both wet behind the ears, that's for sure. We didn't know exactly what we were getting ourselves into. I asked her to tell me her story. She said she was from a small Mississippi town. She had two brothers and was the baby.

I told her I didn't have any brothers or sisters, just my momma. I left out my crazy uncle. I believed the least amount of people to know about him and his despicable ways the better. I decided I'd hold back that bit of news until I knew her better.

We had more similarities than differences, and I was glad she was my roommate. I told her that I traveled here with a friend, and told her all about Josh. I told her we were going to explore D.C. and she would be welcome to go with us.

"That would be great," she said with a smile.

We both started to unpack our suitcases and hang up the little clothing we had. That was something else we had in common—we were both poor.

I took a hot shower, washed my hair, and then fell into bed, exhausted from my traveling. Agent Perry had told me to get a good night's sleep. As exhausted as I was, it was hard for me to fall asleep. I tossed and turned for hours, thinking about Momma, Lauren, and even my stupid uncle. Finally, I must have drifted off to sleep because the next thing I remember is someone pounding on our door and shouting for us to get up.

"You have ten minutes to get down to breakfast," the person yelled. Birdie and I jumped out of bed, threw on some clothes, splashed cold water on our faces, and brushed our teeth. I was brushing my hair as we ran down the hallway toward the stairs to go to the dining facility. I didn't know what room Josh was in at the men's dormitory. I hoped I'd see him down in the cafeteria.

We entered the cafeteria; it was a noisy place with all the chatter and the clanking of plates and utensils. I motioned to Birdie where the line began and we both walked over and grabbed a tray. My eyes grew wide with the choices we had. I looked over and Birdie was just as surprised. We were like kids in a candy store as we told the person behind the glass what we'd like.

We sat in silence as we ate our breakfast. Every now and then I'd search the cafeteria for Josh. After a few minutes, I noticed him sitting at a table with a bunch of young men. I yelled out to him. "Josh. Hey, Josh. Over here."

He looked up from whatever he was doing, most likely talking, and waved to me. I told Birdie, that was my friend, and that I'd be right back. I walked over to where he was.

"Hi, I didn't know what room you were in. I'm in 222," I stammered. All of a sudden, I felt all eyes on me from the table.

Josh, sensing it, too, quickly garbled to me his room number, and then told me he'd "get with me later."

I shrugged my shoulders and quietly walked away. *I guess this is how things are going to play out while we are here*, I thought to myself.

I soon found out there wouldn't be much time for socializing. From the moment we got up in the morning until we went to bed, our time was limited to studying and testing. We also had physical fitness training. We ran laps, did sit-ups, and chin-ups, too.

As we plopped onto our beds at night, exhausted from the day's training, we mumbled a few words letting the other know we were there and share some of the highlights of our busy day. I really was thankful to have Birdie as my roommate.

I occasionally saw Josh but usually at a distance. When we were close enough to chat it was small and awkward talk, an obvious observation that things had changed—and overnight. Sometimes, he and his buddies would join Birdie and me during mealtime, but it wasn't the same. I hadn't expected such a transformation just because we were in training. I tried to rationalize the way he behaved, telling myself that we hardly had any time to do anything but study and train, let alone foster our relationship. I told myself that as soon as we graduated we'd pick up right where we'd left off. I kept a stiff upper lip and acted as if it didn't bother me, but deep down it was killing me. Soon we were hardly speaking. We had shared so much in Texas. We'd told each other our deepest secrets, and now we couldn't even share a meal, or exchange a greeting.

I finished doing my exercises, and Birdie and I hit the showers. It was in the ladies' locker room that I encountered how people would treat Birdie differently than me. They were whispering as we walked by them, and it seemed like they didn't want her to get too close to them—as if her blackness would rub off on them. I watched for a few minutes, and then I yelled, "Didn't your mommas teach you better? We are all humans on this earth, all God's children." I'm not sure where I pulled that from, probably from the Sunday sermons in church that Momma dragged me to, but it seemed to work. From that day forward, Birdie got the respect she deserved, and we even got a few of those ladies, and I use the term loosely, to come over to our side. I'd later discover that, outside my little West Texas upbringing, the whole world had a lot to learn, and especially in some overseas areas.

After the first two weeks of training, Birdie and I sailed through all of our tests. We got our first liberal leave to go into the big city as our reward. Two country bumpkins headed to the big city. Talk about butterflies!

It was a short walk to the metro station. I noticed right away all the different people in my close proximity. It was like a rainbow. Every color under the sun and I was happy to be amongst God's children. Birdie seemed comfortable as well, and that made me more relaxed. I wondered if she'd feel as comfortable if I brought her to my little town. Momma and I'd treat her very nice; we treated everyone nice. However, the display I witnessed in the ladies' locker room told me that some people are not that friendly. Unfortunately, I'd witness many unkind things in my time with the service.

CHAPTER 3

$\mathcal{W}$e stepped off the platform at the metro station, and I, for one, felt like a stranger in my own country. I felt small and confused. No amount of reading in the library could've prepared me for this new and exciting adventure. Birdie didn't say anything, but she, too, had a look of confusion on her face. We walked toward an acrylic stand that held brochures and started looking through them. I had read enough about travel that I knew we needed a map or some type of informational handout. I pulled one out that said Arlington National Cemetery. I searched the stand for other places I had read about, places that Josh and I said we would visit together.

A glossy brochure caught my eye. "Look, Birdie, International Spy Museum. That sounds interesting. What do you think?" At that same moment, she grabbed a brochure that advertised a sightseeing trolley car. Soon we were on the trolley and on our way to the Library of Congress where we would learn that it contained the largest collection of books and other printed material. I was beside myself when we entered the large structure. Not just books, maps, and sheet music were cataloged, but sound recordings as well.

The most somber place we visited that day was Arlington National

Cemetery. The Tomb of the Unknown Soldier, and of course, the grave marker of President John F. Kennedy, left us both speechless. By the time the trolley dropped us off, we were exhausted. Washington, D.C. had a lot of traffic and it took us a lot of time to visit the few places we did. We promised to visit the White House on our next liberal leave day and maybe the U.S. Botanic Garden if time permitted. We rode the metro back to our compound in silence. We were digesting all that we saw; it was a big deal for two small-town girls.

We got back just in time for dinner. We had about twenty minutes to spare before they would close up the kitchen for the night. We each grabbed a tray and proceeded to go through the line, picking the items that sounded good to us. We took our trays to a table near the window. It was dusk, and would soon be dark. We ate in silence and washed our meal down with cartons of chocolate milk. Birdie took our trays and stacked them neatly above the waste container. "I don't know about you, but I'm tired," Birdie said as she yawned.

I nodded my head. "Tomorrow will be another busy day. We have a knowledge test on the history of the State Department," I said.

Birdie and I blew the test right out of the water. One thing was certain—Birdie and I wanted to graduate with excellence so we could start our careers, and travel the world. Birdie and I excelled in every challenge they put forth. We even learned how to shoot a weapon and shoot it well. We had target practice, and both of us hit the center of the paper person every time. We were unstoppable, or so it seemed.

Although I was happy having Birdie as a roommate and friend, I was sad that my relationship with Josh hadn't blossomed like we'd talked about. One minute you're planning your life together—as well as any young person can, and the next minute you're doing something else. I still cared a lot about him, and only wished him well in all his endeavors. I hoped he felt the same for me. I couldn't really know how he felt, though, as he hadn't really given me the time of day since we stepped out of the car that brought us here.

We were nearing our completion of training in D.C. Birdie and I had one more outing planned for the big city. We set out to visit the last couple of places on our agenda. We were waiting in line to enter the White House when I saw a familiar face. Josh and a couple of his friends were in line in front of us. He was joking, laughing, and having a good time. "Look, there're Josh and his creepy friends," I whispered to Birdie.

"Do you think he will make a scene?" she asked with a serious look on her face.

"If he does, we'll just walk away. I don't have any intention of speaking to him unless he speaks first." I tried to ignore his presence so that I could enjoy the tour. We were able to get through it without any incident until we stopped to get something cold to drink. Birdie and I ordered two tall lemonades. "Look, there's an empty bench over there," I said, pointing as I walked toward it. We'd only been sitting for a few minutes when Josh and his bunch walked up to us.

He made the first move. Looking at Birdie first, and then fixing his gaze on me, he asked, "Did you enjoy your tour of the White House?"

I looked at him for a long time before I responded. Many things went through my mind, but finally I settled on, "How did you know we toured the White House?"

Birdie shot a glance at me that told me she'd hoped I wasn't starting any trouble. I looked back at her calmly to let her know I wasn't.

Josh cleared his throat and responded back with, "I saw you two."

My feelings were hurt. I was devastated beyond words. How could someone I had known for the last two years of my life, who I'd shared the most intimate feelings with, treat me this way? I jumped up from the bench, and reached over and pulled Birdie up. "Come on, Birdie, we have a train to catch," I said as we walked away.

Birdie never spoke of the incident. She knew it hurt me to the very core of my being. First my dad didn't want me, then my uncle wanted me and not in a nice way, and now Josh treated me like he'd never liked me. I was beginning to develop low self-esteem and soon became depressed. I was down in the dumps for a few days when Birdie reminded me of what was important. "Jessica. You have to remain focused. Josh is the one who is an idiot. He is being swayed by those gorillas he calls friends," she said expressively.

I nodded that I heard her, but it didn't really persuade me from believing that some of it may be my fault. "My dad didn't think I was worth it, either," I said solemnly as I played with my hair.

"He was an idiot, too," she said boldly.

I looked up at her. As much as him leaving us had hurt, a part of me didn't want anyone to talk bad about him. "Well, Momma said he did love us, he just loved his freedom more."

"Idiot," she spewed as she got up from the bed and looked out our window.

I joined her at the window. The two of us gazed out. After a few silent moments I turned to her. "You're right, Birdie. I can't let some bad stuff that happened to me a long time ago mess me up forever. Josh is just another bump in the road."

Birdie, surprised by my epiphany, gave me a confused look.

"You know, Birdie, no human on earth can take away my desire for travel, pursuing higher education, or anything else in my search for happiness." As I looked up to the heavens above I added, "God be my witness."

Birdie nodded her head. "Amen to that," she whispered.

The next few days, the dorms were full of high energy. Everyone was talking about the graduation and our new assignments. Birdie and I, along with all the candidates, were eagerly looking over the list of all the places we could go. We were to rank in order our preference where we'd like to go. I was beyond excited. Finally, the time was nearing when we were going to travel abroad. Australia, Germany, China, Japan, Africa, Mexico, the Bahamas. "The Bahamas," I shouted out to Birdie.

"It would be warm. No snow that's for sure," Birdie answered. "I was thinking something more exotic," she added.

I nodded my head. "I guess we might as well pick someplace so far away that it will feel like we're on another planet."

"Like another continent," she laughed.

"Yes, another continent," I agreed.

When we finished, we compared notes. Birdie chose Brazil, Portugal, Chile, and Venezuela in that order. I chose Haiti, Peru, Costa Rica, and Bolivia.

"We didn't pick any of the same places," Birdie said, frowning.

"Well, it said we could pick up to five places. Let's pick the same one for our last," I said, happy to oblige.

We both agreed to pick Africa.

ON GRADUATION DAY, we dressed in silence. We were both a little nervous. We knew we would get our orders after the ceremony. We walked down to the assembly hall and waited as the instructors put us in alphabetical order. Josh was in the front, I was in the middle, and Birdie was near the end of the line. I could recognize his profile from a mile away. One of my instructors told me that I had a great sense of awareness and that I'd make a great foreign specialist or even an agent. I couldn't help but wonder what places Josh had put down. We'd talked about so many places when we were planning our getaway together. I wondered if he'd remembered, and purposely selected different locations. I guess I'd find out soon enough.

One by one, they called our names. I wished Momma could've been present. Some parents did make the trip, but most of them didn't travel as far as Momma would've had to. I told her when I called the night before about the graduation. She didn't say much. Momma never said much. However, she said she loved me, and not to forget my manners. "Don't forget where you come from," she added somberly. I assured her I wouldn't. However, I did feel a bit different these days. I was growing up. I was developing my own ideas and, although Momma had instilled many of my beliefs, I'd later discover I was an independent soul.

Everyone yelled and cheered after the director congratulated the entire class. We took a few minutes and shook hands, and hugged those we'd become close with over the last couple of weeks. As I was making my way down the line shaking hands, I came upon Josh. It was awkward. I wasn't sure if we should shake hands or hug.

"Well, Josh, we made it," I said as I looked into his eyes, searching for the Josh I'd known back home.

He nodded his head. "I hope we get a chance to work together."

Taken aback by his comment, I cheerfully said, "You just never know how our paths will cross." I reached up and hugged him. I wished him well, and then I moved along the line congratulating others on their success.

The crowds broke up when the director announced that they were about to inform us of where we would be stationed—something we'd been looking forward to since we signed up. We all got back into our orderly line, waiting for our orders.

One by one, they called our names to step forward. The director handed us each an envelope. "Please don't open it until everyone has theirs," he said to us. After the last person had received their envelope, we waited for the official word. "Go ahead, open," the director said. I was so nervous that my hands were shaking. This is what I had been waiting for since I was twelve; the opportunity to see the world.

Birdie came over to me. We looked at each other, smiled, and then tore open our envelopes. I looked at her trying to find the answer in her eyes, in her expression. I'm sure she was trying to do the same with me. After a few seconds, I offered up the words typed on my paper. "Africa," I said.

"Africa?" she answered back.

I nodded my head. She grabbed me around my neck and squealed into my ear, causing me to lose my hearing for about five minutes. "I got Africa, too!" We jumped around like a bunch of kids, hugging and laughing aloud.

I stopped and placed my hands on her shoulders. "You realize that was our fifth choice?" Birdie smiled. We chatted with our classmates and found out that a few others were also going to be traveling to Africa with us. We were happy for the company. Going to a strange place with fellow graduates would be nice.

Josh came up to us and said he heard we were going to Africa. I didn't want him to think I didn't care, so I nonchalantly asked him where he was going. His body language and the twinkle in his eyes told me he was beyond excited about his assignment to France.

We'd talked about that being one of our dream places when we were sixteen years old. I guess he still found the lure of France to be romantic. I couldn't disagree more. I didn't want any of the places we had talked about. I wanted a new lease on life, and I was about to get it. I wished him well, and then I walked away. Josh was my last link to the little town in West Texas. I outgrew him in a way, too. I didn't know it at the time, but I was going to be thankful that he blew me off in the dining room that day.

CHAPTER 4

*B*irdie and I stayed up all night the night before we were to fly halfway around the world. I guess we finally nodded off sometime after three o'clock. We both awoke bright-eyed and bushy-tailed. We went through our usual morning routine, but the butterflies I felt in my stomach were anything but normal. Birdie was harder to read. She didn't show her emotions, and later I'd find out it was because she didn't want any attention drawn to her. She didn't elaborate, but I think it was because of the color of her skin. I liked her just the way she was.

We were to meet downstairs for our last meal at the training facility. We also got the added bonus of collecting our first paycheck. I had never earned any real money. Back home, occasionally Momma would let me keep a quarter or sometimes, even fifty cents when we would sell our produce at the market. When I ripped open the *official business* envelope and saw my name typed in the "Pay to the order of" space, I got a warm feeling deep inside. I looked to the right of the check and saw the dollar amount. I clenched the envelope and brought it to my chest. I was on my way now. Six hundred and eighty-two dollars and forty-two cents. Holy cow, I was rich.

The State Department was very organized with how they transported us to the airport. I was very impressed. Four large buses lined up, taking us to various airlines at Dulles Airport. Birdie and I boarded bus three. We were flying Delta Airlines. Our ticket showed we would be flying into Entebbe International Airport, approximately thirty-four kilometers from Kampala where we would be living. We checked our luggage and proceeded to filter through the international check-in. We had to show the attendant our passports.

"Kampala, Uganda," he said to me as he looked at my ticket, and then back to my picture on my official passport. I nodded my head.

"Have a safe trip," he added as he waved me through.

I paused for Birdie, but she was right behind me. We both walked down the massive walkway toward our gate. We were early, but that was okay. I took some of my earnings and purchased two books at the airport bookstore, to help pass the time on the long flight. I also bought some candy, nuts, chewing gum, and one of those soft travel pillows that cradled your neck. I felt like such a grown-up, buying my own sundries and traveling by myself. Birdie purchased some magazines and some food items, too.

"Aren't you going to buy a book to read? It's a long flight. You'll finish those magazines fast," I added as I grabbed them from her to see what she'd bought.

Birdie shook her head. "The only book I need, I have right here," she said as she patted the black leather cover of her Bible.

I nodded my head. "I do believe they'll play a movie, too."

"That's what I overheard some of the others saying," she added.

"The last movie I saw was with Josh. We went and saw *American Graffiti*, starring Richard Dreyfuss and Ron Howard."

"Ron Howard, I love him in *Happy Days*," she said with a laugh.

I agreed with her. "My momma and I'd watch that show together," I said gloomily, remembering Momma home alone.

Birdie, sensing I was about to become a downer, got my attention by pointing out the planes lined up on the tarmac. "Look at all the planes, Jessica," she chirped. We walked over to the ceiling-to-floor windows to look at the massive aircraft, one of which would take us to Uganda.

We were about to embark on a mission that we could've never dreamt about, even in our wildest dreams. I wondered if Birdie realized how huge this was.

"I can't believe it. I think I need you to pinch me," I told her.

Always the jokester, she reached over and pinched me.

"Ouch," I proclaimed as we both erupted in laughter. "How can you remain so calm?" I asked.

She shrugged her shoulders. We continued down to the gate area, and finding our place, we sat down in the plastic chairs, waiting for the announcement that told us it was time to board. We'd been sitting for about thirty minutes when an airline employee announced that we'd be boarding soon. Birdie and I found our seats. We didn't have any carry-ons except for our jackets and purchases from the gift store. We took our seats and waited for further instructions. It was only the second time either of us had flown; our first trip being to Washington, D.C. We went over the emergency landing and oxygen mask procedures, which was a little intimidating. I looked over at Birdie to see if she showed any signs of insecurity. Calm as a cucumber, just like Momma.

Except for a little turbulence that caused a bit of nausea, the plane took off without a hitch. I thought I'd have to open the small paper bag that was neatly tucked in the seat pocket before me. I wished my nausea away, and the rest of the flight went great. I dozed for about two hours and would've probably slept longer, but the flight attendant woke me.

"What can I get you to drink, sweetie?" she asked kindly.

"I'll take a Pepsi," I responded.

Birdie and I snacked on our goodies and drank our Pepsi. It seemed like every couple of hours the flight attendant would come by offering us something to drink. After several hours, we were served dinner. I liked the airplane food, and so did Birdie. After dinner, they showed the movie *Blazing Saddles*. Birdie and I laughed so hard. The last several hours of the flight, we read, slept, read some more, and slept again. The flight attendant informed us we'd be landing soon. I grabbed Birdie around the arm. "Did you hear that, Birdie? We're landing!"

"Jessica, calm down," she said, laughing at me again.

Entebbe International Airport was more sophisticated than I had envisioned. We made it through customs all right and found our way to baggage claim. We could hear different languages spoken, and some accents that were more familiar to us. I heard British accents, German, and many other types of languages. I also heard African-speaking people. The tone, and how the words rolled off their tongues fascinated me. We found our two badly worn and tattered suitcases and began to look around for signs showing us the way to a bus, or a taxi.

While looking around, Birdie casually said, "I thought someone would be here to pick us up."

"That would've been nice. I mean look at all these people. I don't know where to turn to," I said, exasperated.

About that time, I saw a guy holding up a sign with our names on it. "Birdie, look, there *is* someone here to get us."

The ride to the U.S. Embassy was loud. The bus we rode in was ancient, and it made all kind of noises as it rolled along the bumpy roads. The town appeared to consist mostly of old structures. Some new construction was taking place, but overall, it looked like a third world country. However, I could see the progress in Kampala that would make it the shining star of Uganda someday. Coming from our little dust bowl of a town, I appreciated the efforts the people of Kampala were making; it would only add more charm to an already charismatic place.

I had done some research on Uganda, and the embassy. The Kampala Embassy's goal was to promote democracy and human rights, ensure regional stability, support health initiatives, and spur economic development—all things I was very passionate about. I was enthusiastic beyond words to pull my sleeves up and get to work promoting all the same, core values as the U.S. Embassy. I also discovered that Uganda bordered Kenya to the east, and on the north, by South Sudan.

To the west, she bordered the Democratic Republic of the Congo, and southwest by Rwanda, and, finally, the south by Tanzania. And at one time, it was occupied by the British. Our bus driver's name was Henry, his skin was darker than Birdie's was, and he spoke with a British accent. He gave all the bus occupants a brief history lesson on Uganda.

After traveling a while, we pulled up to a large compound. Guards were standing on either side of the entrance—a black wrought iron gate inserted between stucco walls. Each guard had a large gun slung over his shoulder. I was a little intimidated by their appearance but after looking around at the rest of the bus riders, I could see that my fear was unfounded.

One of the guards got on the bus and asked us all for our passports. One by one, he looked at the little blue books that said "Passport" with our pictures, and compared the person to the image, or vice versa. I smiled at the guard. Birdie did as well. I noticed the guard was a little smitten with my friend, and I told her so later.

She brushed it off, saying she wasn't interested. "I'm not here to fall in love, Jessica. I'm here to make a difference. See how the other side lives," she added.

I nodded. I realized she was right. Men should be the last thing on our minds. We were all ushered into a large conference room, where officials briefed us on our new positions and our new living arrangements. Birdie and I were so excited.

"Welcome, newcomers. My name is Denton Campbell and I am the compound's human resource officer. I trust you all had an uneventful flight."

The crowd nodded and mumbled some words.

"Let's go over a few things. I know there will be many questions, but let's get you settled. I know you must be exhausted."

Birdie looked over at me; I smiled. It had been a long flight, but I was anything but tired. Birdie and I got the keys to our dormitory rooms. They would be home for us for the next three years. It was a large building with three floors. We were right down the hall from one another, and that made us both happy. Once inside the room, I took a quick inventory—a bed, a tall dresser with five drawers, a nightstand complete with a lamp, and a small bookcase along one of the walls. Along the other wall was a desk and a chair. I opened the first door and it was a closet. The second door I opened was the bathroom, with toilet, sink, and shower—my very own bathroom. I was delighted. I sat on my bed and contemplated everything that had happened during the last year.

I had graduated high school, been accepted into the State Department's career program, and now I was sitting on the bed of my very first apartment inside the Kampala Embassy. I knew it wasn't really an apartment, but it was close enough for me. My own bedroom and bathroom! I was on my way, and I had money in my pocket, which made it all the better. Denton had told us during the newcomers' orientation that there was a bank on the compound and that we should open an account. We would inquire about it in the morning. Just as I was in deep thought, there was a knock on my door.

"What do you think of our living quarters?" Birdie asked as she brushed past me, taking a spot on the bed.

"I think they're great," I said with a big grin.

She nodded her head. "Yes. They really are. Want to go check out the compound?" she asked as she got up from the bed and made her way toward the door.

I hadn't witnessed Birdie this outgoing or curious before. I was intrigued by her behavior.

The compound had a cafeteria, where we would get all our meals. A small dispensary for non-emergent illnesses was also available.

"They will take you to the local hospital in town for more immediate attention," Birdie told me.

We discovered a small post office where we could get stamps and other mailing items. There was also a long wall of post office boxes where we would get our incoming mail. Birdie and I filled out a card so we could get a box. We found a small store that carried toiletries and some food items. There were rows of candy bars, and potato chips, and coolers with soda. Our eyes lit up when we saw all the goodies. As we walked around, we found an activity center with pool tables, ping-pong tables, and pinball machines. Music piped in from speakers hanging from the ceiling and gave it a club feel. Birdie and I had never been to a club before, but we'd read about them. There were tables and chairs strategically placed, and in the far corner, a small bar with a popcorn machine and drink dispensers.

"Do you think they have parties here?" I asked Birdie.

"Maybe," she concluded.

We both decided that our new home for the next three years was more than adequate. We only had to find our new office. Birdie, assigned to the Finance Department, located her building first. I was going to be an assistant in the Educational and Cultural Affairs program. My building was just a few doors down from hers.

"Okay, we both know where to report on Monday," I said to her, walking back toward the cafeteria. "Let's go grab a bite to eat."

The cafeteria was similar to the one we'd had during training. We grabbed a tray and proceeded to tell the food workers our choices. We found a table and sat down. We ate our food in silence, taking in all the hustle and bustle of the room. We could tell that many of the people had been here for a long time and had made friends. There were laughter and boisterous discussions taking place at the tables surrounding us. I was happy to be among them, even if I didn't know anyone yet. Of course, that was about to change. Birdie and I developed many friendships during our assignment in Kampala.

CHAPTER 5

$\mathcal{J}$ settled into my room for the rest of the evening, in preparation for my first day in my new office. I looked through the few items of clothing I had and decided on my only pair of black slacks, and white buttoned-down shirt. I got out my shoes, black patent leather loafers, and decided that would have to do until I went shopping. I wondered where I'd go shopping for all of my necessities while here. I read a little, and then finally dozed off to sleep, dreaming of what my first day in the office would be like.

The alarm clock woke me at five forty-five. I quickly popped out of bed, showered, and dressed. Birdie and I had coordinated that we would meet in the dining facility at six thirty for breakfast. I ran a brush through my hair, and then pulled it back into a ponytail.

Birdie and I were extremely excited about our first day on the job. She was such a whiz with numbers that she was a perfect choice for the Finance Department. She'd be good at a lot of things, but she liked to crunch numbers. I was excited about the opportunity to work in the Educational and Cultural Affairs section. I had a deep appreciation for different cultures, and the goal of the U.S. government in Kampala, among other things, was to promote democracy and human rights, areas I was passionate about as well. We ate in silence, both of our minds focused on our new jobs. We gave each other a hug and promised to meet for lunch.

"Don't worry about a thing, Jessica. You've graduated at the top of your class, you're dedicated, and there is nothing you can't do."

I grinned and then nodded. "I'm just a little apprehensive, is all," I said coolly.

Birdie squared her shoulders and stood tall. "See you at dinner-time," she called out as she happily walked toward the building that housed her new office.

I slowly made my way toward the building I'd be working in, casu-ally looking back at Birdie until I saw her go in the door. I hesitantly opened the door to the two-story building and went inside. I saw a wide-open space, with cubicles and desks. People were sitting and chatting. People looked up at me as I made my way to the back of the room, looking for my supervisor's office. I smiled at the people as I kept walking, and when someone spoke to me, I greeted them back. I stopped in front of a door with a nameplate on it; it read "Mr. Phillips." I gently knocked, and waited for someone to say it was okay to enter. I then heard, "Come in, the door is open." I gingerly opened the door, and sitting behind a large wooden desk was a man I presumed to be Mr. Phillips.

"You must be the new hire," he said as he rummaged through papers to find my name.

I cleared my throat. "Yes, I'm Jessica McCarthy."

"Yes, Jessica. I'm sorry. I'm a bit disorganized," he said apologeti-cally. "Welcome to Uganda."

"Thank you," I uttered.

We went through all the standard small talk stuff—where are you from, what is your education, and the like. He told me he'd lined me up with a buddy.

"Someone who has been here for a while, who can show you the ropes, and get you acquainted with Kampala, etc.," he said as he got up from his swivel chair. I followed him out to the central area.

"Staff, can I get your attention for a minute?" Everyone in the room turned around to look at us. "This is Jessica McCarthy. She is our new specialist. Please give her a warm welcome." Cheers and clapping erupted, and as I looked around the room, I felt the warmth of many smiles and sincerity surrounding me. I knew I'd be happy in Kampala.

After the warm reception, a young man walked up to Mr. Phillips and me. "Hi, I'm Bitalo. I've been asked to help you get settled in," he said as he extended his hand to me. I took his hand in mine and shook it gently.

"It's nice to meet you," I said, both cautiously and politely.

Mr. Phillips turned around, went back into his office, and closed the door. Bitalo showed me to my desk. It was right next to his. I was quietly taking it all in. I guess Bitalo thought I was disappointed in my desk since he quickly broke my concentration. "We're field agents, so we don't spend a lot of time sitting at our desks, except to write reports," he added. "Have you had a chance to look around the compound?"

"Yes, my friend Birdie and I looked it over yesterday."

"Good, let's just take it slow for a couple of weeks, but in the future I'd love to take you outside those metal gates for a look-see," he said as he smiled.

I loved his smile, and his gray eyes made him unique like me with my own owl-like eyes. His smile was contagious and I found myself grinning and nodding as he gave me the ins and outs of the office. "I really do like my desk."

Smiling from ear to ear, he responded with, "Good."

Bitalo's English was perfect. "I guess you learned English while at university?" I asked.

"No, we speak English here, and it is taught in the schools," he corrected. "However, we also speak a few other languages, and one you'll hear me talk in is Swahili."

"Swahili?" I probed.

He nodded his head. "Yes, Swahili."

"What does your name mean?" I asked, waiting for some wonderful description such as seeker of faith, or brave one.

Bitalo laughed. "Well, you're going to get a laugh out of this." I grinned at him, waiting for the answer. "Fill in the blanks ... Kentucky Fried Chicken is ..."

I had a puzzled look on my face. I thought about it for a second and then replied, "Finger-licking good?"

Bitalo belted out a boisterous laugh. "Yes. It means finger-licking."

We both erupted in laughter. As we walked around the compound, Bitalo filled me in on a few things. He was indeed a *local* from a nearby village. He was educated in Kampala for primary school, and then he attended the Kampala International University for his undergraduate and graduate degrees. I felt a little inferior, just having my high school education, although I knew I could hold my own if we discussed anything I had ever read in a book—and I had read plenty. He told me his parents were educated, as well, and both his parents were schoolteachers. Impressed by their accomplishments, I acknowledged how proud he must feel to have successful parents. I told him about my momma and our lonely existence in West Texas. Even though I didn't think it was much to brag about, he thought it was awesome that we grew our own food and lived off our land.

"We have something in common. The people here commonly grow their own food."

I believed he really was sincere, so I began to tell him a few more stories about my home, but nothing about my uncle.

"I don't want to overwhelm you on your first day, Jessica. Let's go outside for a brief tour of the grounds. Mr. Phillips asked me to show you around. You may have missed some things," he said, smiling as he pushed open the door.

He led me around to the various spots that he thought were important. Birdie and I had indeed missed some, so this was good. "Over there are the post office, small convenience store, and sports bar."

"Yes, Birdie and I did come across those places. We filled out the paperwork to get a post office box, too," I said modestly.

"These four buildings," he said, pointing to our building, Birdie's, and two others, "house the functional operations of this compound."

We stopped walking for a moment so that we could talk and give each other our full attention. "Finance, Education and Cultural Awareness, Security, and Administrative Support," he reiterated, "are housed in these four buildings."

I nodded that I understood. We continued walking.

"Over there, beyond those trees," he said, pointing, "is the dispensary. Minor cuts, sprains, and the like are treated there. For emergency medical treatment, you would be sent by ambulance to the big hospital near the city center."

I didn't have the heart to tell Bitalo that Birdie and I had already staked out these places. We continued walking some more when Bitalo pointed out the small library, another small café, and a tiny theater. "We aren't limited to staying here," he said. "We can go into town as well. I'd like to take you out beyond the iron gates soon, Jessica, if that's okay with you."

"Of course, you can take me out into town. That would be great," I added.

That night over dinner, I filled Birdie in on my first day, and Bitalo. I couldn't stop going on and on about him and his almost perfect English when Birdie finally stopped me with her rolled eyes and disgusted look. "I'm sorry, Birdie. I've rambled on so much about my day and haven't let you get a word in about yours."

Birdie laughed. "My day was not as eventful as yours, that's for sure. However, I did meet some nice people who I think could be potential friends."

We ate the rest of our dinner in silence, but my mind drifted to my great day with Bitalo. I knew we would become great friends. We'd had some sort of connection. I couldn't wait to introduce Birdie to him. I knew she'd like him, too.

CHAPTER 6

*L*ife was anything but dull in Uganda. I was busy learning my new job, meeting new people, and learning about the culture. Birdie and I had great discussions in the evenings over dinner. Our meals were actually good. Some of them would remind us of back home, while other foods were prominent in this part of the world and new to us. I learned to love cassava, a tapioca pudding.

Bitalo continued to help me grow in my new job as an education and cultural specialist. I had to learn about the many customs of Uganda, including the one I'd have the most difficulty in observing— being subservient to men. You see, women's roles were subordinate to those of men's. In small villages where education was still a luxury for girls, they were to *know their place*, and that meant kneeling to men. I had a real problem with that. However, I wouldn't rock the boat in a country that was a temporary home for me. I quizzed Bitalo on some of the customs. He was an educated man, so his perspective on this interested me greatly. We had long talks about some of the customs and cultural differences between his country and mine. He said that he liked the idea of a woman being his equal.

After about a month of not leaving the compound, Bitalo asked me if I wanted to venture out. "Sure, that would be great," I told him enthusiastically.

"Kampala has some very nice shops. It would be appropriate for our first *field trip*," he said in his very proper English.

I met him at the office, where we went over a few ground rules. "Remember, you're a guest in our country. Most men of the older generation are not going to give you the respect you deserve. However, many younger men have been Western educated and influenced. You'll know the difference. Just follow my lead," he added.

I nodded my head that I understood. My palms were sweaty and my stomach was doing flip-flops. The anticipation of what I'd see beyond the gates left me filled with anxiety. We made our way outside the iron gates. Kampala was a busy city, bustling with activity everywhere I looked. The sights, sounds, and smells of the street market congested with women, men, children running and playing with balls and sticks, and the occasional stray dog, suggested a community in chaos. Add bicycles into the mix, and it was almost impossible to get around. Vendors selling their wares dotted the sidewalks and they could set up shop in any open space.

The constant billows of dirt and dust from people and vehicles and the smoke from all the burning, soon had me coughing. However, the lively raw energy of Kampala was everywhere, and the pushing and shoving of the many people browsing the wares almost seemed natural after a while. I couldn't get over the stifling poverty, though. I'd never get used to that.

In the distance, a small wooden display with brightly-colored scarves caught my eye. Bitalo noticed that I was observing them.

"All the women love the scarves. Do you want to go look?"

"Okay, if you think it would be all right," I said timidly.

I walked over to the makeshift stand and admired them. I reached out and gently took a scarf in my hand, appreciating the colors and the feel of the fabric between my fingers. One by one, I searched through the many that were on display, finally deciding on one with variations of green. Just as I was to make my selection, I felt a wet nose on my leg. I quickly turned to see a spotted mongrel giving me nose kisses!

"Is it okay to pet the dog?" I asked Bitalo.

"Yes. However, be sure to wash your hands afterward. Some of the dogs here have mange and other diseases."

That little bit of information was enough to tell me to steer clear—and I was a sucker for animals and kids. Turning my attention back to the scarves, I settled on the green one. I was excited about sending it to Momma. We walked a bit farther and I saw a man selling silver and gold jewelry. I thanked him for letting me look at his merchandise. Bitalo said something to the man. I'd later learn that he told him that I was new to the area and he was showing me around. After about an hour of walking around and looking at things, Bitalo asked if I'd like to get some tea.

"I know a little café around the corner. They have good tea and cookies made from yams. You'll like it."

I shared my experience that evening with Birdie, as I had done with all my news since we'd moved here. I think she was a bit envious, as she had not ventured into town yet. Her work buddy had not offered to take her yet. "I bet it will be soon," I told her, trying to lift her spirits.

Birdie got her chance for a visit into town just a few days later. She was excited and had stories of her own to tell. I listened intently as she had for me. That's what good friends do for one another. She bought a beautiful scarf for her mom, too.

I was listening to Birdie give details about her trip into town when my mind wandered off the topic at hand. I wondered how Lauren was doing in college, and Josh on his assignment in France. I thought about them both for just a few minutes when Birdie caught me drifting from our conversation.

"You're not listening to me!" she said disgustedly.

"I am, too. Just for a split second, I drifted. I couldn't help but think about Lauren and Josh," I said forlornly. "I wonder how they're doing, and what they're up to," I added.

Birdie grumbled something about them worming in on her time. I just laughed it off.

I WANTED to get involved with a charity.

Bitalo shared with me the various opportunities available to help the local villagers. I was to become familiar with the programs, as it was part of my job to know the culture of the people, and how best to serve them. The mosquito netting endeavor, as well as building schools and churches immediately intrigued me. I knew that girls didn't attend school as regularly as boys, so building more schools was important. Girls, I felt, should have the same opportunities to learn skills and become leaders. Africa's overall development depended on it. I also knew how important mosquito netting was for preventing malaria. I only had time on my hands, and my weekends were boring and long. I decided I could do both.

Birdie, being the great adventurer she was, agreed to help me. Birdie had not met Bitalo yet, but just as I had hoped, they hit it off. As we drove the Jeep deep into the countryside, Bitalo provided background regarding the project we were to help with. He told us that a group of missionaries was involved in the project as well, and he'd be introducing us to his friend, Andrew.

CHAPTER 7

$\mathcal{A}$fter our first introduction, I knew there was something unique and special about Andrew. The way he gently shook my hand, the way he paid full attention to my every word, and the eye contact ... the eye contact almost made me feel uneasy and made my stomach tighten and the hair on my arms rise, giving way to goose bumps up and down my arms. It didn't really matter what it was that drew me to him, but I was drawn for sure.

Andrew wasn't at all like Josh. He was refined and cultured—from his years living abroad, and I found myself lured by his charm. His suave behavior had me captivated, and Birdie and I both seemed to hang on his every word. We agreed that it was partly due to his British accent, but also because he had a worldly feel about him, one we couldn't really put our finger on. It also didn't hurt that Andrew's physical attributes were anything but average.

He was about six feet tall and had reddish-blond hair and languorous green eyes that made me melt. He had a few light brown freckles on his cheeks, which gave his face a warm glow. He was what I'd call a pretty boy. Nevertheless, he was anything but girl-like. He was a man's man all the way. His hands were callused like Momma's, along with some cuts and bruises on his arms, all signs of his hard work. I loved the smell of his clothes, a combination of sweat, dust, and perhaps a faint whiff of an aftershave lotion. I'd later nickname him *gentle giant*. It had a strange, quixotic ring to it—the owl and the gentle giant.

I'd get up early on Saturdays and be ready for Andrew to pick me up outside the iron gates at seven o'clock. We would be gone until seven or sometimes eight that evening. I thrived on the mission of getting those nets out to the villagers, but I thrived more on Andrew's energy. I loved being with him. On the two-hour drive to the villages, we would get to know one another. He'd never been to the United States, but it was on his *bucket list*. He never tired of asking me questions, and I never grew tired of answering them.

His father, a missionary, got Andrew involved with the organization at a young age. He arrived in Uganda at the age of twenty-two; his parents were assigned to another area of Africa, near Rwanda. Every story he told me was like an adventure, and I hung on his every word. He did the same with me. He'd listen intently as I told him the stories of June bugs and fireflies and of days spent lazily strolling along the creek beds looking for treasures. I told him we were poor and my only way out was to dream big. The way he'd stroke my hand convinced me it was going to be all right. I was happy to find someone I could confide in, tell my stories to … like I used to do with Josh.

Birdie and Bitalo became fast friends, and soon they were inseparable. He even took her to his village of Jinja and introduced her to his family. She had a lot to say about that. She told me that his parents were very kind, and his mom was especially sweet to her. Being teachers, they didn't seem to practice the concept that men were superior to women. That was good, in Birdie's case. She wanted to be respectful, but she didn't have it easy growing up in the South as a black child. She worked her buns off in school to graduate at the top of her class, and she didn't want to stifle her accomplishments—especially to men.

"I was glad to see that his parents do not believe that men are superior," she told me pointedly. I nodded. "I did bow my head a little when I shook his dad's hand, but I did not get down on my knees," Birdie revealed. We both laughed after that one.

Birdie told me of the great meal she'd had with Bitalo and his family. "Chicken stew with vegetables—I think sweet potato was in it, and millet bread—oh, and tapioca for dessert," she added, smiling. Birdie had a great appetite for deliciously prepared food!

"Sounds delightful, Birdie," I replied. I was glad that Birdie was getting out and having fun with Bitalo. I was happy we were both getting out. This is what we dreamed about and worked so hard to accomplish while in training—traveling to faraway places and making a difference, no matter how slight, in our little spot of the universe."

"Where is Andrew taking you next?" Birdie asked.

"He said something about a wildlife reserve," I said, beaming.

"You mean lions, tigers, and giraffes?"

Nodding my head, we both cried out, "Oh my," breaking out in sidesplitting laughter.

"I don't know exactly when he's planning this, but it's on the schedule. I love the way he says schedule in his British accent." I pronounced it for Birdie, putting the emphasis on the c and h and running right past the s. We laughed at my imitation of Andrew. It was all in fun.

We both agreed to call it a night. Birdie wanted to read a few verses in her Bible, and I had a book I was reading, too; a romance novella about a cowboy and a ranch hand's daughter. We bid each other good night and made plans to have breakfast together. As we walked up the the stairs and eventually the hallway that would lead us to our rooms, I gave Birdie a hug. She stared at me after we separated.

"What was that for?" She wanted to know.

"That's for being my friend. It would be a lonely world without you," I added genuinely.

"Ahh. You're the best, too. I'm glad we were roommates back in D.C." She then lowered her head.

"What's wrong?" I asked her.

She slowly raised her head, looking me squarely in the eyes. "I don't want to think about it, but someday we're going to go different places," she said solemnly.

"Taking the positive approach," I said, "let's not talk about that now. Let's enjoy our time together—here … now."

I got ready for bed and settled in to read a few chapters of my novella when there was a knock on my door. Not being dressed for visitors, I grabbed my bathrobe and answered the door. It was another dorm resident letting me know I had a phone call. "Who is it?" I asked, stunned to get a call at night. The first thought that ran through my mind was Momma. "Some man," is all she said. I hurried to where the only phone was located for our entire quarters. There, I saw the receiver dangling by the cord waiting for me. I nervously picked up the receiver and held it to my ear for a second or two, before I spoke. "Hello? This is Jessica," I said with an element of alarm.

"Hi, Jessica, it's me, Andrew."

I let out a sigh of relief, worried deep inside that it was my uncle calling, telling me something had happened to Momma.

"Andrew, why are you calling me so late?" I asked, scared that something had happened to his parents.

Sensing my tension, he quickly followed his greeting by letting me know why he was calling.

"Well, I was thinking about you. I guess the truth of the matter is, I didn't want to go to sleep until I heard your voice," he said gently.

I smiled into the phone. "Ahh, Andrew, you're so sweet. I don't know what I've done to deserve you, but I, too, am happy that you are in my life. I'll see you soon. You plan that trip to the wildlife reserve. I can't wait to see that," I said, wrapping up the phone call.

"Okay, I'll do that."

We hung up, and I wandered down the long, dimly-lit hallway to find my room. I didn't hear any sounds coming from the other rooms. I hoped I wouldn't receive any complaints about my late-night phone call from my boyfriend. Boyfriend! I liked the sound of that.

I didn't get much sleep. I tossed and turned thinking about Andrew. The phone call may have helped him sleep, but it did anything but that for me! I awoke the next morning feeling as if I'd been run over by a train. With bags under my eyes, and a slight headache coming on, it would be a rough start to the day. I was looking forward to a good breakfast with Birdie.

"Wow, you have some major dark circles under your eyes, Jessica!" Birdie reported.

"Andrew called me last night!"

"Was it an emergency?" she asked, looking for answers.

"No. He merely wanted to tell me good night," I said, embarrassed.

Birdie smiled, revealing her cupid's bow lips. "He really is smitten with you, Jessica," she said.

"I was worried something bad had happened, but all he wanted to tell me was how happy I make him."

"I'm glad that you two are getting along so well. Bitalo and I are having a great time as well," she said, letting me know that I wasn't the only one with a gentleman caller.

"I care about him, that's for sure. I enjoy being with him, and I think about him often. The way he looks at me is as if he can look deep into my soul." I uttered. She nodded.

Birdie didn't have much to say after that. We finished our breakfast in silence and went our separate ways to our respective offices.

I was working on a few outreach projects regarding cultural awareness. I was nervous about doing a good job. It was my first major task as an education and cultural specialist.

I had already become somewhat known in a few of the villages when I helped with the mosquito netting project, and now the school project. My job was to get out into the communities and spread the word about the many opportunities we could assist with. I developed an action plan to help teach gardening. I had plenty of experience; Momma had the greenest thumb when it came to gardening. I felt I had natural talent, and was excited about the opportunity to help start community gardening in a nearby village. I hoped that it would catch on and that other villagers would want to do the same.

I did the research to find out what would grow best in Uganda's soil and climate. I compiled a list and went through the supply person to order the many packets of seeds and tools I'd need. On my way back from placing my supply order, I overheard the group making dinner plans. I wondered if they would invite me. I was plugging away on my project when Bitalo came over to me and filled me in on the plans. I wasn't sure if I felt up to going, but after a few seconds of hesitation, I accepted. I knew Birdie would worry if she didn't see me at dinner. We always had dinner together.

We had such a blast with my co-workers. They were so much fun to be around. Birdie and Bitalo were quite the item all evening, huddled together, and whispering as if they were the only two in the room. I wondered where their relationship was headed. Birdie had once confided in me that she was not interested in falling in love. She didn't want anything to stand in her way of traveling the world and experiencing all that was out there. I had agreed with her view then. But now I was having feelings for Andrew, and I wondered if it would stop me from pursuing my dreams.

Bitalo was kind enough to walk us home. It was dark out, and although we were within the walls of our compound, it wasn't one hundred percent secure from uninvited guests. I felt safe with Bitalo. I know Birdie did, too.

"Here we are, girls," Bitalo said.

"Thank you for walking us home," we both said at the same time, laughing at our timing.

I could tell that Bitalo wanted to say something just to Birdie, so I excused myself and entered our building. I lingered a while in the hallway, walking slowly, hoping she'd come bopping in and catch up to me. I kept walking, but no Birdie. I finally reached my room and went inside. My mind traveled to many places regarding the two of them. I wondered if he was kissing her, telling her some wild story about Africa, or perhaps he took her away! My heart was pounding after my last thought, but just then there was a light tap on my door. I rushed to it and swung it open. There stood Birdie with a look on her face that told me I was, at least, right about one thing.

"All of a sudden, he leans in and kisses me!" she tells me, adding, "Ravenously." This was a different side to Birdie than I had witnessed before.

"Calm down, Birdie. Sit," I said, pointing to the bed.

She began to tell me how he looked into her eyes and expressed what a wonderful time he'd had with her during dinner. I nodded my head for her to go on. She said she didn't even know what sparked the kiss. "He just did it. I didn't have any warning."

I asked her how she felt about the kiss. "Did it give you goose bumps?"

"Goose bumps, chills running up and down my back, and the hair on my arms stood straight up!" she exclaimed. We both laughed at her description.

"I'd say that was a damn good kiss, Birdie!" We laughed again. It was hard for me to go to sleep again, and I could only imagine what Birdie was doing. She was probably wide awake or dreaming of Bitalo. I was happy for her. She was a great person and deserved happiness. We all did.

MY LIFE in Kampala was exciting. I often wondered how many people could say the same about their life. I was beginning to fit in with my co-workers, and was soon tagged as *Go get 'em, Jessica*. I was constantly thinking of projects that would help the community.

Bitalo and Andrew were planning our game reserve trip. Lake Mburo National Park was the closest to Kampala and would be our first stop. The four of us got along well, and Birdie and I were blessed to be doing what we loved and loved who we were doing it with!

BIRDIE and I packed large floppy hats to keep the sun off our heads— the African sun gets hot—a scarf to help keep dust out of our mouths, and canteens full of water. I wanted to take pictures but didn't have a camera, and neither did Birdie.

"Let's stop over at the store here on the compound. I saw cameras one day when I was looking around," she said confidently.

I purchased a small Kodak camera and a roll of film. I promised Birdie I'd get copies made of the pictures so she could have some. Birdie had her eyes set on a pair of binoculars. She wasn't sure about spending the money. She was saving for something big. She hadn't told me yet what that something was.

"Buy the binoculars, Birdie," I appealed. "Those binoculars will help us to see some of the animals up close," I added.

Andrew and Bitalo had made plans to meet at the compound's motor pool to secure a Jeep for us. Birdie and I waited outside for them. I was very excited about what we were going to see. We chatted nonstop and before we knew it, Bitalo was pulling up to park at the reserve.

"Don't forget your camera!" Birdie reminded.

"Don't forget your binoculars!" I bantered.

We were met at the gate by one of the reserve staff. They directed us where to park our Jeep, and told us where to meet for the guided tour. As we waited for the tour guide, we got acquainted with the people who would be sharing our vehicle as we drove through the savannah. We only waited about twenty minutes, but it seemed like hours.

The tour guide was friendly and presented a detailed overview of what we would see. He told us some of the animals we might encounter: zebras, warthogs, buffalo, impalas, and eland, the largest of African antelope! He cautioned us to stay in the vehicle at all times and to obey all of his commands. Although he didn't anticipate any disturbances, he said wild animals can be unpredictable, and our awareness of this fact would keep us safe.

"Get your camera ready!" Birdie exclaimed. I laughed at her.

"I've got it all loaded and ready to click away," I assured her.

The Jeep was an exact replica of those I'd seen in magazines and books, with olive drab paint and roll bars with a canopy over the top to keep the sun off us. The driver helped us one by one to take a seat on the worn leather bench seats in the safari-type vehicle.

The tour guide answered our countless questions. He told us the history of the game reserve, and going over again what we might see, when all of a sudden out of the tall grass came a warthog with a lion running fast behind it. The driver stopped the Jeep suddenly so we could watch nature in action. The power and grace with which the lion ran were very impressive—the warthog, not so much. However, it ran like there was no tomorrow. They disappeared into the thick brush. I hoped for the best for the little warthog, but something deep inside told me otherwise.

"Did you see that, Jessica?" Birdie squealed.

"Yes. I couldn't capture much on film. They were moving too fast for me. I'm afraid after we get the film developed, it could be just a blur," I said, disgusted.

We'd traveled a little further when we came upon two lion cubs. As we watched the playful antics of the cubs, we forgot the golden rule: where there are baby animals, mothers are nearby. Just at that moment when everyone was oohing and aahing, a large female lion gingerly stepped across our path. She looked at us for a moment and then directed her attention toward her cubs. We all sat frozen, not speaking a word. Only the sounds of faint breathing could be heard and the beating of my own heart. The lioness growled, letting her little cubs know it was time to go, and off into the tall brush they ran.

"I can't believe what we just witnessed!" I said, shaken by the experience.

"I never get tired of seeing animals in the wild, and Mother Nature at her finest," Andrew said as he stroked my hand, trying to calm me down.

The driver continued along the dry and dusty road while the tour guide continued with his presentation. As we anticipated what we'd see next, our adrenaline began working overtime—keeping us on edge. As the Jeep rounded a bend, we came to a clearing and just beyond—a large lake. Playing in the water were several elephants, spraying each other with water from their trunks. I was able to snap several pictures.

"Aren't they cute?" I said.

"Cute?" Andrew chuckled. "I'd say majestic is a better description," he said, teasingly.

I agreed. The elephants were indeed magnificent.

After a few moments, the driver continued. This time, we came upon a herd of zebras grazing in a large field. They were swatting the flies off their rear ends just like the cows back home. They didn't seem the least bit afraid or interested in us.

I'd have to say that all the animals amazed me in one way or another, but when we came upon a group of giraffes, I couldn't believe how tall they were. We watched in amazement as several of them stripped the leaves off the tall branches, as we took pictures.

The tour guide announced that our adventure would soon be over, and wanted to know if we had any questions. Birdie and I were still taking in everything we saw, and unfortunately, it would be after I retired to my room that I'd think of many questions to ask. I vowed that on my next visit to a wild game reserve, I'd bring a pen and notebook!

As we traveled on the road that would lead back to the main entrance, the tour guide called out to us. There was a huge flock of migratory birds that had made their home at the reserve. I made a mental note to purchase a bird book to see if I could identify any with my pictures. This was an excellent educational opportunity for us. I had read about safaris in books, but this was real life—and no book could adequately describe the gratification one felt seeing the animals in their natural environment.

Andrew reached over and took my hand. I looked up at his sweet face dotted with freckles, his red hair that hung across his forehead and down his eyebrows almost getting into his eyes, and my heart melted.

In his lovely British accent, he said to me, "I just love it out here, so peaceful and serene; animals living off the land in their own habitat, as they should."

I nodded. It was so true. I couldn't have said it any better.

After a very long, but wonderful day at the Lake Mburo National Park, we headed back to the compound. We had nibbled on the snacks we took with us, but we were ready for a meal. We all agreed we could eat a horse. Realizing that probably wasn't the most appropriate thing to say, having just visited a game reserve, we found the humor in it anyway and erupted in laughter.

As we finished our meal and our time together was nearing its end, I reflected on many things. I'd come so far in the last couple of years. I thought about the many times I sat under the big oak in our yard in West Texas and dreamt of the day I'd be in places such as Kampala, Uganda. I guess if you'd asked me back then, I would have said it just helped pass the hours—dreaming of faraway places. It wasn't until Josh told me about the State Department program that a glimmer of possibility started to show through.

If you want something bad enough, you do whatever you can to make it happen. I was happy that Momma had instilled these qualities in me. Thinking back, that's why she was able to let me go. She would've never stopped me from becoming successful.

On the way back to the dormitory, the four of us chatted nonstop about our day. Each of us took something different from the experience, but the one thing we all agreed on was that we'd had an incredible time together, and vowed to do it again soon.

Soon Bitalo and Birdie walked past us into the shadows of the building. It was dark out, and I couldn't see where they'd gone. Holding hands and casually talking, Andrew and I stopped near the entrance to the building. Every now and then I could hear Birdie giggle. I imagined they might be kissing.

"I had a great time with you, Jessica." *The way he said my name!*

"I had a wonderful time," I said, making my adjective sound more important.

He pulled me in closer. I didn't resist—I found myself knowing just what to do. It seemed natural, and the next step in the order of things. At the same time, we unclasped hands, and I put my arms around his waist, while he put his hands on my shoulders.

"May I kiss you?" he asked self-consciously. I nodded. He hesitated for a brief second, and then he leaned in. His mouth was soft and warm, his kiss gentle like the soft, warm wind that blew through West Texas. After a couple of seconds, he broke away. I could've gone on kissing him longer—I was just getting into it.

"That was very nice."

"Yes, it was," I responded, sad that it had ended so quickly.

"I really enjoyed being with you. I hope you have a lovely evening. Do you have any plans for next weekend? I wanted to know if you wanted to help me at the new school site. We've got the walls up and could use help painting," Andrew said.

"Yes, I'd love to help paint. I'll meet you there Saturday morning."

He reached in and hugged me, and I responded, hoping he'd decide to kiss me again. I didn't want to let go.

Just about that time, Birdie and Bitalo rounded the corner and came upon us. We broke away from the hug when we felt their presence. All of us giggled a little, and then said our final good nights. Birdie and I walked into our building.

"Jessica, I had the best time today!"

"I did, too! Andrew is such a sweetheart. I'd never have met him if we hadn't come to Kampala!"

"I'm thankful you introduced me to Bitalo," she said, hugging me.

"You're welcome, Birdie," I said, hugging her back. "You know, I had my eyes on him first, but figured it wouldn't be wise to date one of my co-workers!"

Birdie jabbed me in the ribs. "You better keep your eyes on Andrew," she giggled.

CHAPTER 8

*A*fter living in the city for almost a year, I was beginning to know my way around pretty well. I had mastered the antiquated bus system that took me to nearby villages where I volunteered during my days off. Every chance I got, I helped Andrew with one of his many projects. He had his hands in everything, or so it seemed. That's what I really liked about him—his ability to give selflessly and do it so wholly.

I arrived at the construction site early on a Saturday morning, after traveling for almost an hour on an old bus, that frankly, I wasn't quite sure would even make it. It sputtered and squeaked, and it sounded like a huge tin box as it hit every bump in the road along the way. I was feeling a bit nauseated when I finally got to my destination. The bus's exhaust fumes trapped me like a prisoner in my seat. I couldn't seem to get away from the smell. I opened the windows, but the blue-tinged smoke just hung like a fog, rolling into my space. I was happy to get off that old bus and breathe some regular air. I'd say fresh air, but actually, the air is pretty thick in Africa in the summertime.

Andrew was busy hammering nails, but he saw the big bus pull up to drop me off. I saw him put the hammer down so that he could greet me. "Hi, Jessica!"

"Hi, Andrew. I didn't think I was ever going to make it in that old tin box," I said, laughing.

"Yes. The buses around here are a tad vintage," he said in his charming British accent.

"I'm ready to work; where do you need me?" I said enthusiastically.

Andrew handed me a paintbrush and put me in a room with a couple of local villagers. It was quite an experience, painting with the village women. They laughed, sang tribal songs, and teased me endlessly about Andrew. Love truly was a universal language. After we had painted for a couple of hours, the ladies left to prepare lunch. I sought out Andrew to see if I could be of any more help. I helped the construction crew by gathering debris and tossing it into large metal containers that would later be disposed of. Thanks to many generous donors, supplies and equipment were not an issue when it came to building this school, or, as I'd later find out, any school.

The ladies provided an excellent lunch of local delicacies—fish grilled to perfection, matoke, a staple made with bananas, and tea. After we had filled our bellies, we went back to work, painting and putting the finishing touches on the little schoolhouse.

I was getting ready to dip my brush in the bucket of paint when a little puppy about six months old caught my eye. He was malnourished and appeared a bit lethargic. I remembered Bitalo cautioning me about dogs and diseases. I guess I threw caution to the wind that day. I reached down to pet the little dog who, for obvious reasons, I later named Spot. I made sure he had water and food and soon he became the mascot for the little schoolhouse. Every day that I made the trip out to the site, Spot would eventually show up for his daily pat on the head and special treat. The teacher promised me Spot would always be well cared for.

After an exhausting, but a gratifying day, Andrew put me back on the bus that would take me to the compound. He asked me if I wanted to attend church services with him on Sunday. I hadn't been to church since I'd left Texas. I agreed it would be nice. He said it was within walking distance, so we arranged to meet outside the gates of the compound.

"Ask Birdie and Bitalo if they would like to attend as well," he said as he helped me up the steps of the bus. He didn't kiss me that day, and I found it a bit strange. I wondered about it all the way home and hoped it wasn't something I had done to discourage him from trying to kiss me again.

The church service was held under a huge canvas top, much like a circus tent. Inside, rows of white plastic chairs filled the area. We found some seats and we waited for what could be described as a very entertaining service. In churches back home, the choir was accompanied by the organist. Here in Uganda, drums replaced the organ. Soon everyone was tapping their feet, and some were so moved by the music that they began to dance in the aisles. It was a different experience than I was used to, and Birdie, too, for that matter. I looked around and Bitalo and Andrew both were very comfortable in the church setting.

THE SCHOOLHOUSE WAS TAKING shape and nearing completion right around my second anniversary of living in Kampala. I remember the event well. We were furnishing the classrooms with desks, pencils, and paper, mounting large chalkboards and stocking the shelves with textbooks. I recall to this day how I was bursting with pride to be part of such an accomplishment. I think of Andrew and me, side by side, painting the outside of the school in a shade of schoolhouse red. I have fond memories of Birdie and me planting native vegetation along the building, and Bitalo hanging the brass bell that the teacher would ring to let the children know that school was in session. Many times throughout my career with the service, I'd think back to those great times. The monumental sacrifices that Andrew made as a missionary, serving the great people of Uganda, would forever leave an impression not only in my mind but also deep in my soul.

The first day the little school opened, the four of us were there to see the smiles on all the girls' faces as they stepped through the door. Looking back, I don't know who was the happiest—the girls, their moms, or us. It was a step in the right direction, and Birdie and I were so pleased to be part of it. Andrew grabbed my hand and held it for a long time. I looked at him as he gazed devotedly at the completion of yet another immense undertaking. His chest puffed up with pride, his face beaming. I was very proud, too. I'd later realize that his work would always come first.

After the schoolhouse doors had closed, the four of us walked to the bus stop where a rickety old bus would take us back to the compound. Andrew was staying behind just to make sure everything ran smoothly during opening day. For the most part, the community accepted the school, but sometimes, a few community members would protest. Andrew didn't anticipate any trouble, but just in case, there were also a few armed guards standing nearby. Armed guards didn't bother me anymore, but I recalled feeling differently the first day Birdie and I arrived at the compound, and they had boarded the bus looking at our identification. It seemed so long ago.

"When am I going to see you next?" I asked Andrew as I held on to his strong arms.

"I don't know, Jessica. I've been asked to travel to Johannesburg next week to look at a site for another school. I'll be gone for a while."

I was surprised by this news, as he hadn't mentioned anything about it. "Oh, I see," I said uneasily.

Andrew could sense that I was a little upset about the sudden news of him going away. "I'll be back before you know it," he whispered as he hugged me close to his chest. I could feel the beating of his heart against my ear. It should have brought me comfort, but instead, it brought me anguish. I wondered if we would be together all the time. I should have known it was temporary. His life as a missionary would take him to faraway places. Thinking that he'd always stay in Kampala was a mistake on my part, one I'd have to learn from, unfortunately.

While Andrew was away, Birdie, Bitalo, and I promised him we would check in on the girls at the school. He wanted to make sure that the community continued to support the missionaries' efforts in educating the girls. He feared that perhaps boys would take over the classrooms. I vowed that I wouldn't let that happen.

For two weeks, the three of us bagged our lunch, eating it on the bus that would take us to the school. Satisfied that all was well, we boarded the bus again for the trek back to the compound.

Mr. Phillips was very kind and understanding when Bitalo and I were a few minutes late returning to the office. He said to consider it part of our outreach, and for us not to worry about being a little late. On the other hand, Birdie's boss wasn't quite as understanding. "That witch docked me twenty-five minutes!" Birdie informed me later that evening. It didn't stop Birdie from going with us the following days.

She felt as strongly about the girls getting an education as we did. "It's only vacation time she's docking me. Heck, we can't go on vacation here anyway. That'll be reserved for when we go back to the States," she added, slightly disgusted with her supervisor.

Birdie gave me an idea about using vacation time in Africa. "Why can't we use vacation time here?" I asked. "We've earned it; we're entitled to use it." When Andrew returned from Johannesburg, I'd surprise him with my idea of accompanying him for a little R & R.

I heard it first from Bitalo at the office that Andrew was back in Kampala. I waited for his call. After about two days, he finally contacted me. I was excited to hear all about his adventure, and what extraordinary mission he was doing in Johannesburg. We made plans to have dinner together at a local café.

Andrew told me all about his trip. You could see the excitement in his eyes as he spoke about the groundbreaking for the new school. He explained that a well-known talk show host in the United States, who avidly supported causes such as this, was providing the financial backing for the construction of this particular school. Everyone was abuzz, hoping they would get to meet her. I grew even more excited about the possibility of meeting someone so famous and decided now was the time to let Andrew know I could travel with him. The look on his face when I told him said he, too, was happy to have the company. I told him I'd get it all squared away with Mr. Phillips. "I plan to go back in five days," he said, slurping his tea.

I had a lot to do in the next few days. I had to get my leave approved by Mr. Phillips, pack a few items, and ask Birdie to water the one houseplant I had in my room. I hoped she wouldn't be too involved with Bitalo and forget to tend to my only request.

As anticipated, Mr. Phillips approved my request for to take some vacation time in five days. I was so excited to be traveling with Andrew. He picked me up in front of the gates to the compound bright and early. I had packed some sandwiches for our trip. We sang songs, played word games, and of course, he asked me all about Texas. I'd already told him so much about it, but he seemed never to get bored of the details. We had such a great time traveling. We finally arrived at our destination late in the evening. Tired, hungry, and dirty, I couldn't wait to retire to my accommodations. Andrew parked the Jeep and helped me out. "Your tent is over here," he said, signaling to a large military issue-type tent.

"I didn't know we were sleeping in tents," I said, trying to sound optimistic, but not pulling it off too well.

He laughed at my surprise. "It's really not that bad, Jessica," he said scornfully.

I didn't really believe he was that disgusted with me, it was more of his British brashness coming out. He lifted the flaps of the tent and we walked inside. A cot, blanket, small wooden table with a wash pitcher, and a trunk filled the tent.

"Your accommodations for the next five days," he said proudly.

I slept like a baby, a crybaby, that is. I constantly worried that wild animals were going to come into my tent and eat me alive. If that wasn't absurd enough, I worried about natives who didn't like Americans and how they might circle my tent and put a spell on me. I had one vivid imagination, and I was glad when I saw the warm streams of sunlight beaming through the openings in the tent. It couldn't come soon enough for me.

"How did you sleep last night, Jessica?" Andrew inquired.

"Let's just say, I didn't sleep too well," I retorted as I looked around for a warm beverage to drink.

"I'm sorry you didn't sleep well," he said, hugging me close to him.

I could feel the tone in his muscles from the hard work of his chosen calling, building churches and schools, that I'd come to admire or love. *Love? What was I thinking? It's a little too early for that!*

I'd hardly finished digesting my breakfast of biscuits and hot tea when Andrew thrust a hammer into my hand.

"Time to get to work," he said, walking away toward the structure. *Not even a peck on the cheek, huh?* I thought to myself as I followed him.

We worked from early morning to late at night. I wondered where Andrew and his crew got their stamina. I was worn out already, and it was just the first day for me. I guess their drive came from the enthusiasm they had for their project. That was certainly important. Momma always told me that if you don't have a goal you just stumble through life. I guess she had a point. I developed serious calluses on my hands from driving the nails into the wood with my hammer, and pulling out the crooked ones that I bent when I didn't hit the head accurately. Andrew wanted it perfect. When I could hardly hold my hand up to drive the final nail of the evening, and my head was heavy with sleep, Andrew said it was time to quit for the night. "Tomorrow will be here soon enough," he told the crew and me.

We headed over to the camp and washed up. The local women were kind enough to prepare dinner, and I, for one, couldn't have been happier to know my dinner wouldn't have to be fixed by me! We sat around a makeshift table and chairs and before we ate our dinner, Andrew said grace. I bowed my head and listened to his blessing. He blessed the food we were about to eat, and he asked for our safety as we tackled the project of building the school. For fun, he also asked if we could meet the famous talk show host who was backing the project. Everyone laughed at that.

The next four days were a lot like the first one. Early to rise, work all day, have dinner late, and fall into bed. After I had been there a week, I was getting a little anxious to get back to the compound. I had fun helping Andrew, and I absolutely believed in the cause. I just wasn't sure if I wanted to give up my life for this type of work, day in, day out. I had a lot of soul-searching to do, that was for sure. I loved being with Andrew, and we had a lot of fun together, but something was missing in our relationship, and I couldn't quite put my finger on what it was. I was hoping on the long drive back to Kampala I'd be able to immerse myself deep in thought, and maybe come up with an answer.

Andrew dropped me off at the entrance to the compound. I had only a small bag, so I was able to maneuver it well enough. I walked through the gates, flashing my identification to the guard, and walked toward my billets. I stopped by Birdie's room to see if she was there.

"Tell me all about Johannesburg!"

"Well ..." I stammered. "I didn't get to see much of the city. Andrew put me to work the very next morning. Look at my hands, Birdie!" I said, showing her all the cuts and calluses.

"Yuck! That looks like it hurts."

"The good news is we accomplished a lot in the week I was there. We slept in tents, and the local women fed us," I added, trying to be thankful for something.

"Well, I'm glad to have you home where you belong," she said, smiling.

I threw myself into work, and diligently pursued the many projects I was handling for our office. I didn't think of Andrew too much, surprisingly. Occasionally, I imagined him on ladders, hammering nails, and doing what construction workers do. I thought of them sitting around the big wooden table at mealtime and saying blessings. I guess I did miss a few things, but I didn't miss sleeping in the tent! I occasionally would ask Bitalo if he'd heard from him just so someone thought I missed him. However, the truth of the matter was that I was missing him less and less.

CHAPTER 9

*A*ndrew didn't return to Kampala for more than thirty days. By the time he returned, I almost forgot what he had looked like. He apparently had forgotten about me as well, as we acted more like friends, or even siblings than boyfriend and girlfriend. I'd been down this road before, first with Josh, and now with Andrew. It was okay with me how things turned out. He was happiest traveling around Africa, building churches and schools, and I was just as happy supporting him from the sidelines. It wasn't in me to join him, after all.

I was happy for the opportunity to help where I did, and I think I made a difference, not only in the lives of others but my own as well. I was a restless soul, though, and I knew I'd joined the service to travel the world, and nobody was going to hold me back, not even Andrew.

I had heard the rumors that it was time for rotation. I knew I'd get my official letter from Washington soon. It was just as well that Andrew and I ended our fling when we did. Birdie, on the other hand, was totally smitten with Bitalo. She did exactly what she said she wouldn't do—she fell for him like a ton of bricks.

"What are you going to do when you get your letter that says you're moving to the Azores?" I asked, not being very supportive.

"I'm not going to be sent to the Azores, Jessica! I've asked for an extension to stay here for another year."

"Really?" I asked, surprised.

I guess Birdie's plans changed after developing a relationship with Bitalo. I was okay with the fact that she'd found someone she cared enough about to change her plans. I guess that's what lovebirds do—they plan their life together. I was happy for them, really I was, but I couldn't wait to explore the world. I waited on pins and needles for that official letter. It wasn't long after that discussion with Birdie that I received my new assignment.

I knew it was coming, but it still surprised me when I opened my post office box and saw the envelope. I panicked for a brief moment, not really sure why. I picked up the letter and looked at it long and hard before folding it and putting it in my pocket. I decided to head back to my room where I could read it in private.

I slowly walked back to the dorm, and as I walked, I thought about how that folded letter would change my future. Once I got back to my room, I sat on the bed, and gazed out across the room, looking out the window. Finally, after about five minutes of wasting time, I tore the letter open.

The letterhead said from the Secretary of State, Washington, D.C. I read the first paragraph.

To Miss Jessica McCarthy,

This is to inform you that on May 12, you will report to Frankfurt, Germany.

"Frankfurt, Germany," I said aloud. I jumped up from my bed and hollered, "FRANKFURT, GERMANY!"

I tore out of my room, running down the hallway, making a beeline to Birdie's room. I rapped hard on her door, waiting for her to answer. It felt like minutes, but after just a few seconds she opened the door, a towel in her hand, and a look on her face that told me she knew I had gotten my letter.

"Come in, Jessica," she said, opening the door for me. "Where are they sending you?"

"Guess," I responded, playing with her.

"Japan?"

"Nope, guess again."

"Hawaii?"

"No, guess again."

"Okay, Jessica; this is the last guess. If I don't get it right, this time, you spill the beans, do you hear me? Italy?"

"No! Not Japan, not Hawaii, and not Italy," I said pausing just a bit before I hollered, "Germany!"

"Germany? Wow. That should be interesting. I think they drink a lot of beer there," she said laughingly.

OVER THE NEXT SEVERAL WEEKS, I arranged my departure from Uganda. I coordinated with the moving people to have the few things that wouldn't fit in my suitcase shipped in a total of three boxes to Germany—things I'd purchased as mementos of my time in Africa.

I could tell that Birdie was feeling some anxiety about me leaving. I made a mental note to try to have some alone time with her so we could talk.

As with everything that is good and exciting, time slipped away and my departure from Kampala came quickly. I captured a few moments here and there to express to Birdie how I would miss her. We talked about all of our time together and laughed at some of our earliest memories together in Washington, D.C. We both agreed life would be different without each other, and we vowed to stay connected.

My office threw me a going-away party. Bitalo brought Birdie along, and although Andrew was invited, he was off on one of his visionary missions. He gave Bitalo a letter for me. On the outside, it read, "Don't open until you're on the plane." I figured it was a Dear Jessica letter, and not caring what it said, tossed it into my bag for later. I was more concerned at this point about how I was going to hold up when it was time to say goodbye to my two dear friends, Birdie and Bitalo. They'd stood by me the entire time I lived in Kampala, and I'd miss them.

I never thought I'd be leaving Uganda without Birdie. We'd always talked about our next assignment together, but instead, she was staying behind. We made plans to reunite somewhere, to use that vacation time we were earning to see each other again. I knew the chances of it actually occurring were slim, but nevertheless, we promised to try.

The day finally arrived when I had to say goodbye to Birdie, Bitalo, and the place I'd called home for the past three years. The two of them walked me to the bus stop. We made small talk, avoiding any discussion of my leaving. Once we arrived at the bus stop, I put my bag down, and reached over and pulled Birdie to me, hugging her hard and long. We didn't say anything to one another. The tears were already forming on my lower lids and slowly dribbled down the side of my face. I heard her sniffle, letting me know she was crying in silence, too. After a few moments, we pulled apart.

"I don't know what to say, Birdie. The words just won't come out," I said, looking down at the ground.

"I know ... I'm having a hard time, too. But, on the bright side, you're going to Europe!" she said in her always-upbeat fashion.

I let out a small giggle, trying to find the humor in anything. The bus pulled up, and people started getting off while others got aboard. "Well, here's my bus. Time to go," I said sadly. Birdie nodded.

Bitalo came over and gave me a big hug and a peck on the cheek. "Jessica, it's been a pleasure working with you and having you as my friend."

"Bitalo, thank you for everything. You take care of my friend, okay? I'd sure like it if you came and visited me," I added as I made my way toward the steps of the bus.

I boarded with my one bag in my hand and casually turned to see my friends one last time. I blew them both a kiss and with a heavy heart, I made my way down the aisle of the bus, locating an empty seat.

Once I was on the bus, I was okay. The hard part was over. I'd soon be at the airport, and the next chapter of my life would unfold. The door to the bus closed and as it made its way down Main Street, I waved goodbye to my friends until I couldn't see them anymore.

I arrived at the airport with time to spare. I thought about the letter from Andrew. I waited as Andrew had asked, and didn't tear open the letter until the pilot announced we were cruising at fifty thousand feet.

The plane was rather noisy, so I figured it would be okay to read it, and if I shed any tears or made any sniffling sounds, they'd be drowned out by the cabin noise. The neatly folded letter had a faint scent that reminded me of him. I took a moment and let the smell linger, traveling up my nostrils, giving me chills that ran down the back of my neck. I let out a sigh and decided to continue with the overwhelming burden of reading my Dear Jessica letter.

I KNOW you're confused about what happened between us. I'm just as confused if that makes you feel any better. I really enjoyed being with you, and under different circumstances, we probably could've made a go of it. Right now, my work as a missionary is very important to me, and sadly, I don't have room in my life for someone as wonderful as you. I know you'll find happiness in your new assignment in Europe. Always be careful, and always be you. I hope we'll meet again someday, and perhaps, pick up where we left off. Safe travels, my little amber-eyed beauty.

IN FONDNESS,
   Andrew

. . .

I CLOSED up the letter and neatly put it back into the envelope. I wasn't sure what I was going to do with the letter. I'd hold on to it for a while, and when the time was right, dispose of it.

The minute I stepped off the plane onto the tarmac at Frankfurt, I knew I'd traveled to a great place. Immediately, I noticed that the air was fresher, the sky bluer, and the energy of the people was contagious.

I'd discover that the Germans were hardworking and resilient, characteristics I found admirable. They worked hard, and they played even harder. I was in the right place! I stumbled into the metro station adjacent to the airport. With the help of kind local residents, I located the right train and soon was on my way to the embassy.

As the train clattered along the tracks, I enjoyed the beautiful scenery. Everything was so green, and unlike Uganda, there were plenty of rolling hills. Living in Germany would prove to be quite different than living in Uganda. The poverty and devastation I saw on a daily basis in and around Kampala were not evident in or near Frankfurt. Instead, I witnessed quaint cottages, little villages, and as I got closer to Frankfurt, I saw a bustling economy with major businesses and numerous cars on the road. Besides the obvious economic bustle and the weather, my living arrangements were also quite different than when I'd lived in Uganda. Unlike Kampala, civilians stationed in Germany lived on the economy.

The embassy was located in the heart of Frankfurt, and I was in awe of the beautiful city and the many historical architectural designs that it housed. The clean-swept streets and sidewalks, the numerous cafés and bakeries that dotted the city, and the friendliness of the people equated to a great second assignment. I checked into the embassy as my orders had dictated, where I received a map and a list of possible hotels to stay until I secured a permanent residence.

I decided on a hostel instead of a high priced hotel, saving money to go toward my apartment. I wanted to be within walking distance to work, and near the excitement of the downtown area, and I was quite sure that convenience would come at a premium price.

I got a good night's rest and reported to work early. I wanted to make a great first impression. The embassy was beautiful, and the compound overall was grand. The Consulate General of Frankfurt, as it is known, is the largest U.S. Consular post, and one of the biggest diplomatic missions in the world. Also, it served the American residents community, including members of the armed forces. With the busiest international airport in the world, it played a crucial role in providing services and support to hundreds of U.S. missions around the world.

The Consulate, I found out, was also a major regional conference and training center for staff from other embassies and consulates. This compound was one busy and vital operation. Things were so different here in Deutschland. I wasn't sure how my job as an educational and cultural specialist would fit in. I'd find out soon enough.

I checked in with the personnel office. I was being assigned to the Public Affairs office and, after a series of interviews, I was placed in the support function as an administration specialist within the Amerika Haus.

The Amerika Haus was an initiative that began the creation of small libraries throughout Germany with books donated by American soldiers at the end of World War II. After the libraries were established, the U.S. government and the cultural affairs section, specifically, continued with the efforts in support of facilitating dialogue on political, economic, and social issues. The cultural affairs section co-sponsored seminars, lectures, and other programs in cooperation with German partner organizations.

A serious library patron in my youth, it was the perfect opportunity for me. I must have had a special angel looking after me; I had the perfect job in Kampala, and now in Germany. I was ecstatic.

I immediately felt comfortable with my new role as an assistant in the Cultural Affairs Department. My co-workers were from all areas of the United States and several foreign countries. I was immediately drawn to one of the girls in the office, named Crystal, who later would become my friend, and coincidentally be my next-door neighbor. It made it very convenient for our friendship to not only work together but also live close by. We had a lot in common.

The apartment was located three blocks from the embassy. It was in the attic of a German family's home. It had a small kitchen, a bathroom, and a large room that served as the living room and bedroom. A large Murphy bed pulled out from a large mahogany cabinet, and at bedtime, the living room transformed into my bedroom. I had my own key to their main door, and the stairs led straight up to the attic. They also lived on the second floor, so sometimes I had to make sure I was quiet, especially if I came in late at night. There was so much to do and see in the Frankfurt area that I was hardly home. I loved my little apartment, and the German family was very kind to me.

THE YEAR WAS 1977, and the world lost a great performer; Elvis Presley was found dead, at the age of forty-two. I was twenty-one years young, and The Bee Gees and Rod Stewart hit the circuit both in the United States and abroad. Movies such as *Rocky*, and *Close Encounters of the Third Kind* were top at the box office. The ever-delightful polyester pantsuit, complete with a tunic top and bell-bottoms, was on every fashion magazine cover.

The scene in Frankfurt was hip, pop, and funk. I totally got the vibe, and to demonstrate that I got it, I purchased my very own pantsuit in a vivid green. I loved all the funky little nightclubs that played blues, jazz, and tried to imitate groups like The Beatles. I liked drinking hot coffee in huge white ceramic cups, all the while thumping my feet to the music. It wasn't just Germans who visited these places, but also tons of Americans.

There were military bases all over the Frankfurt area, and with a strong American presence, international performers were endless. That's how I met Grayson. He was attending a gig at one of the smoky little clubs known for producing new talent in the arena of comedy, song, and poetry. I was sitting at a table with a few of my co-workers, and he was sitting at a table adjacent to ours with three of his friends. He kept looking over at me, and I couldn't stop looking at him. He was gorgeous with a capital *G*. After a few song sets, he got up and came over to our table.

"You must be new. I know everyone who comes here, and I don't recall ever seeing you."

"I've been in the country for about a month. I've been to this place twice," I added, fidgeting with my napkin, wondering what exactly to say next and avoiding eye contact.

"Would you like to join my friends and me?" he asked as he nodded toward their table.

"Thanks, but maybe another time. I'm here with my friends tonight."

He grinned, nodded his head, and then silently walked back to his table. I watched him as he made his way back to his friends. He was about six feet tall, with broad shoulders, sandy brown hair, and light brown eyes. *I guess I'd gotten a better look at him than I'd thought!* I'd hoped I hadn't made him mad. That was not my intention, but I thought he was bold in assuming I'd sit with him after just meeting him.

After the last performer, we left the club and started the walk to our respective apartments. One by one, the group went their separate ways, leaving Crystal and me to walk the rest of the way alone. The streets were still busy, and people were walking all over, so we felt comfortable walking home despite the time. We'd walked about two blocks beyond the rest of the group, and were just rounding the corner of the block that would take Crystal and me home, when I heard a familiar voice. "Hey, new girl!"

I stopped and turned around and saw Mr. Gorgeous running up behind us. He should have startled us, two young women walking alone, but for some reason, we both felt he was harmless enough.

"Yes?" I queried.

Nodding to Crystal, he then turned his attention to me. "I didn't get your name."

"I didn't give it," I said staunchly.

"My name is Grayson Fuller," he said as he extended his hand toward me.

I took his hand and gave it a light shake. "Jessica McCarthy, and this is my friend, Crystal."

"Can I walk you two ladies home?" he asked as he started walking, not waiting for our answer.

Realizing that he was going to walk us home regardless, I shrugged my shoulders, and said, "Sure, we just live about five minutes from here."

We didn't have time for much conversation, but he told us he was assigned to the Army Garrison nearby. I didn't really feel like disclosing too much information about myself, but I did tell him we were assigned to the embassy.

"Do you think you'll be at the club again soon?"

"I don't know. We try out different ones. I might be, though," I added.

We said good night, and Crystal and I walked up the stairs to our humble homes, closing our doors at about the same time. I hesitated briefly before shutting my door, just in time to see Grayson still standing at the bottom of the steps watching me. I quietly closed the door, turned the lock, and walked up the two flights of stairs to my modest little apartment. I have to admit I thought about him for a fleeting moment.

There was so much activity to concentrate on; I was just beginning to discover Frankfurt, and rediscover myself, so I didn't really want to get tied down with a boyfriend. It hadn't worked out so well with Josh, or Andrew. I decided I needed a break from boys!

CHAPTER 10

*C*rystal was born and raised in Germany. She'd never lived outside of her country and found my stories of Texas fascinating along with my accounts of Birdie, Bitalo, and Andrew. I pretty much characterized my childhood as dull, boring, and uninteresting. I told her about Josh and Lauren, and as usual, left out the part about my crazy uncle.

I skipped most of the boring stuff and went right to my first assignment in Africa. Crystal couldn't believe I'd lived there, and found the stories I told captivating, especially my adventure at the wildlife reserve with Andrew. Crystal briefly told me about her own childhood. Her parents, both strict, raised her with a no-nonsense type of parenting. She wasn't given much freedom, and that explained her somewhat promiscuous nature as an adult.

She was a pretty girl with shiny brown hair and lavender colored eyes. I'd never known anyone with lavender eyes except for movie star Elizabeth Taylor. She left home after graduation and chose to attend University to continue her education, and then landed the job with the embassy. She liked working for the government. She hoped one day to travel, but right now she was having fun being carefree.

Crystal and I really hit it off, and on most days we could be found together. We'd have lunch together, take breaks together, and always walked home together. On the weekends, we went out on the town, where she showed me all the great shopping places—where I found my vivid green pantsuit with the bell-bottoms, and all the little cafés and clubs we became so partial to. I really liked Europe, and I'd soon discover places like the Rhine, Nahe, and Mosel Rivers, the Christmas Market, castles, and fests—lots of fests.

For my first overnight excursion, Crystal and I rode the train for four hours to the Bavarian Alps to tour the famous Neuschwanstein Castle. This postcard perfect setting was internationally famous. Built in the late 1800s for King Ludwig II, this fairy tale castle inspired Walt Disney to create the Magic Kingdom castle at his parks. Not only did the castle have a fabulous view from the top of a hill, but it was also advanced beyond its years—having flushing toilets, heating, and air-conditioning systems, and water supplied by a nearby stream.

I was in awe of the mastermind behind this magnificent structure with its exaggerated turrets and grand appearance. I decided to read up on King Ludwig II at the library upon my return.

After an exhausting, but wonderful experience, Crystal and I checked in at a small gasthaus for the night, but not before dining on jaeger schnitzel and pomme frites. Now that I was twenty-one and of legal age to drink, to celebrate our first overnight outing, Crystal and I had a glass of wine from the Mosel Valley, a very nice Riesling kabinett.

Tired and full, the two of us turned in to our comfortable yet modest accommodations. Fortunately for us, many European hotels furnished the rooms with twin beds, allowing us each to have our own. Unfortunately, however, we had to share a bathroom down the hall with the other occupants.

The next morning we awoke refreshed and ready for our trip back to the embassy—but not before having a European breakfast. The coffee was a bit robust, but the food was as wonderful as the night before, and it helped fuel us for our trip home. The views from the train were awesome. I was constantly snapping pictures through the window. I wasn't sure if they would turn out, but it was worth a try.

Miles of picturesque views, quaint farms, and villages, with several lakes and many charming churches dotted the landscape. Green fields with cows, sheep, and the majestic Alps in the background—it was postcard perfect.

I was daydreaming about how my life had changed since I'd left Texas. Sometimes, I felt like I was in someone else's movie or story. Crystal and I talked endlessly about the job, Germany, our families, and of course, men. She hadn't really met anyone she wanted to settle down with. She was too busy having fun.

"If the right guy comes along, I'll give up my playgirl status," she said, laughing.

I found myself comparing and contrasting Lauren, Birdie, and Crystal. Lauren and I were still young and developing our personalities when we were friends. I liked her a lot growing up, and she was a great listener. Birdie was so different from Lauren. She was shy in her own way, but at the same time, could be outspoken. I wondered how far she and Bitalo had gone in their relationship. Crystal, it seemed, was a combination of the two of them. She was somewhat reserved but wasn't afraid to venture out of her comfort zone. It was as if she was analyzing everything before she committed, but that was all right with me.

I tried to see where I fit in with them, in terms of my own personality, and decided that I, too, was a bit reserved. I chalked it up to my small-town upbringing.

We arrived at the Frankfurt train station exactly four hours and fifty-two minutes later. I was tired, as we'd gotten up early. We flagged down a cab, and soon we were home. "I had a great time, Crystal. Thanks so much for taking me to *Mad* King Ludwig's castle."

"You're welcome! Get some sleep; tomorrow is a work day," she said as she climbed the stairs to her apartment.

I nodded. Wanting to show her that I was learning German, I shouted out to her, "Auf Wiedersehen, Crystal!"

~

CRYSTAL and I enjoyed many more trips after that. Some were day trips that took us to neighboring towns and villages where we'd shop a little, eat a little, and sometimes drink a little. Other times we'd take the train, explore, and stay the night. I was learning to like the taste of beer and wine. I knew my momma wouldn't approve, but it was an easy way to dull the sadness I sometimes felt. I enjoyed my job, and Crystal couldn't be any nicer, but I felt like something was missing from my life, and alcohol seemed to make this feeling vanish. Everything seemed a little bit funnier, a little less serious, and time seemed to stop after a few swigs of cold frothy beer or sips of fine German wine.

Crystal and I noticed we were getting a bit pudgy around the middle and contributed it to the beer, wine, and all of the good food we were indulging in. She suggested we take up volksmarching, a form of non-competitive fitness walking. The trails were usually ten kilometers or just over six miles long, and at the end, we were given a pin or patch for our accomplishment. If the patches or pins weren't incentive enough, the beer and food tents were! We justified our eating and drinking as an earned reward for our efforts.

"I don't know if this is helping to trim our waistline, Jessica."

"At least it's getting us moving," I interjected, hoping it didn't sound too much like a cop-out.

It was true; it got us out, and the cost was minimal except for the food and drink we purchased. We both agreed we'd skip the beer on our next walk. Slowly we'd get into shape. Neither of us was trying to impress anyone, but we also knew that keeping our weight down was the best way to live a long, healthy life. Besides, the service didn't want a bunch of overweight special agents, no matter what department they were in.

I WAS PREPARING FOR AN EVENT, which focused on the importance of literacy and the role of Amerika Haus. I loved my job. It was so perfect for me to work with libraries and books!

I was designing some informational handouts that I'd get the printing office to produce when Crystal approached me. We worked in the same office, so seeing her on a regular basis was the norm.

"Hi, Jessica. How's the project going? Need any help?"

"Take a look at this; do you think it's appropriate, or should I add something?" I asked as I handed her the draft of my handout.

"I think it's great, maybe just add a graphic and some color," she added, handing back the pamphlet.

We made small talk, and before she got up to leave, she asked if I wanted to go out to the little club around the corner from our house. "Just to unwind," she added.

WE LOCATED a table for two near the small dance floor. The music for the night was provided by a DJ. The barmaid soon approached our table to take our drink order. "Zwei bier, bitte," Crystal said. We sipped our ice-cold beers as we listened to American music. We'd only been in the establishment twenty minutes or so when Grayson and one of his friends walked in.

Like radar, he immediately locked onto us and made a beeline to our table.

"Hey there, ladies. How goes it?"

I smiled. The music was a little loud, making it difficult to have a real conversation. I directed my attention to the couples dancing. I wasn't really ignoring him, but I wasn't all that interested. Before I knew it, Crystal was asking them to join us. I glared at her, but she just smiled, and in her thick German accent told me to be nice.

Grayson and his buddy pulled up chairs, flagged down a barmaid, and soon they were drinking beer and tapping their feet to the music that bellowed from the speakers. After the second round, the jokes started rolling off our tongues and laughter ensued, letting everyone know that we were having a great time. I noticed that Crystal was getting a bit chummy with Grayson's friend. Soon they were out on the dance floor slow dancing. I was worried that Grayson would ask me to dance; I had two left feet so that wouldn't have been a good idea.

I excused myself to the restroom, hoping it would give me time to think of an excuse for why I wanted to go home. I could see where this was headed, and the beer was making it hard for me to stick to my convictions—not getting involved with any more men!

After I returned from the bathroom, Crystal and Grayson's friend, Charles, were sitting down, laughing and carrying on. I felt as if I was actually intruding. I pulled my chair out from the table and slid in. I sipped the beer in front of me and listened to them tell jokes. When Crystal turned to me and asked if I was having a great time, I gave her a look that told her I wasn't!

I overheard her tell Charles that I was tired and wanted to go home. Soon we were on our way, but not before Charles and Crystal exchanged something that was scribbled on a paper napkin. Grayson and I stood off to one side as they flirted and promised to see each other soon.

"I guess those two really hit it off," Grayson said, nodding toward Crystal and Charles.

"I guess so," I muttered.

"Listen, I think we may have gotten off on the wrong foot," he said as he moved a bit closer to me.

My expression should have told him it didn't matter, that I wasn't interested, but he continued to push me.

"I like you, Jessica. Can't we give it another try?" he asked, looking like a little boy looking for his lost puppy.

I guess you could say I let my guard down. Before I knew it, I was exchanging information with Grayson on a beer-stained paper napkin.

CRYSTAL and I were forming a great friendship. We were having the time of our lives—two single, attractive women, living and working in Germany. I found myself still not believing it some days. It seemed just like yesterday that I was living in a sleepy little town in West Texas, dreaming of the day I'd escape. I couldn't help but think about Momma. I really missed her. I'd been saving up my money, and soon I'd be making the long trip back.

I also found myself thinking about Birdie, and Bitalo, and of course, I thought about Andrew. I wondered if he found anyone worth settling down with. The one person I wouldn't allow myself to think too much about was Josh. I had to admit that I still cared about him. I thought we'd be together until the end of time. I sighed, thinking about all the friends I'd made and lost along the way to finding my happiness. I wondered if I'd ever truly find happiness.

Crystal, Charles, Grayson, and I started spending a lot of time together. The guys had been to many of the attractions in the area, and of course, Crystal had knowledge about many of the same places. We decided to go for a cruise on the Rhine River. I couldn't help but worry how things were going to develop between Grayson and me. I wasn't stupid. I didn't just fall off the turnip truck. I knew that when a guy liked a girl and vice versa, things happened. I just wasn't sure I was prepared for all the drama that it would entail. But, Crystal was really smitten with Charles, and I promised I'd go along on the cruise.

We met the guys at the train station. It was only about an hour train ride to the docks where we'd board. The itinerary included a couple of stops along the river. I was excited to see Philippsruhe Castle in Hanau, the historical towns of Seligenstadt and Aschaffenburg, and the serene rolling hills dotted with vineyards. The region was renowned for their wine. But what stayed with me for a long time were the legendary Loreley Cliffs near the village of St. Goarshausen.

We had fabulous views of the river and everything along the banks. We sat up on top, oohing and ahhing, all the while sipping some of the wine produced from the very same vineyards we were seeing. Soon it was dinnertime, and we feasted on traditional German food that I'd come to love. It had a familiarity to it, even though I'd never officially had it before moving here. Breaded cutlets drenched in gravy, fried potatoes, and salad—seemed like a meal one could get in any part of the United States. However, it didn't taste like anything

I'd had before. And, the desserts—real whipped cream delights, with just the right amount of sugar—not too sweet, followed by a stout cup of coffee. Yes, the Germans certainly knew how to throw a meal together.

After we had dined on the delicious food, we all settled in the main ballroom area where a live band was playing music. It wasn't the typical top 40 music we were used to listening to, but it was music, and it fostered the festive mood we all were in. With drinks in hand, we found a table that would accommodate us and proceeded to sit. Soon, Crystal and Charles were on the dance floor swaying to music that was popular before they were even born.

Having them gone gave Grayson and me an opportunity to get to know one another better. It was obvious that we were clicking with or without the alcoholic beverages. I continued to engage him, hoping he'd open up about his childhood and his likes and dislikes. I mean that's what friends do ... they get to know one another. I didn't know if we'd ever be more than friends, but I wanted to make sure he was, in fact, someone I'd like to be around and get to know better. As we were in deep discussion, I noticed Crystal and Charles had left the dance floor, no doubt to get some fresh air.

"Did you have any pets growing up?" I asked out of the blue.

Looking a bit startled, he quickly responded. "Yes. We always had a dog and couple of cats, and I even had a few hamsters in my time."

"I never had a pet. We couldn't afford the food and veterinary bills. But ... we had cows, and my best friend, Lauren and I loved to ride our bikes down to the creek and watch them swat flies off their rears with their tails!" I told him, laughing at the thought of those beautiful creatures.

"I always wanted a horse, too, but Momma said we could barely afford to feed ourselves, let alone a large animal like a horse. We did have some feral cats that I'd occasionally sneak a bowl of milk to when Momma wasn't looking."

"Animals are great to have around, but they do require care and money. Someday, when I'm out of the military, I will have some," he added.

Now I knew where he stood with animals. He loved them!

I was just about to tell Grayson how much I enjoyed his company and how I thought we were getting along fairly well when an announcement came on from the captain that we were close to our destination and final stop. I played with the straw in my drink, wiping the sweat from the glass, and finally eating the maraschino cherry that garnished the glass, trying to not be obvious that I wasn't actually drinking any. Grayson didn't even notice that I didn't finish it. We collected our things and made our way to the gathering place on the boat where we'd be getting off soon.

The boat pulled in and docked. Everyone got off in a very orderly fashion. I figured some of it had to do with the alcohol, and some of it had to do with the mere fact that it had been a very pleasurable after-noon, and although many didn't want the day and evening to end, it ended on a high note. We caught a cab that took us to the train station. We didn't wait long for our train. The German railway system is excellent and has an incredible record of timeliness.

While on the train, I found my gaze fixated on Charles and Crystal; I could see that they were getting closer by the moment. I knew she'd had a few boyfriends. We talked about it from time to time. I told her about my first love, Josh, and how he'd disappointed me, and it seemed from that point on, all the guys had hurt me one way or another. I guess, truth be told, I didn't have a good track record with love. I'd been lured by fairy-tale promises before, only to find out that not every prince is charming!

We were soon getting off the train and making our way home. Charles and Crystal were going to her apartment together. I didn't want to give Grayson any ideas, so I told him up front. "Listen, Grayson," I finally got out, "I had a great time, and I really like you, but …"

"But … here comes the but," he said, sounding dejected.

"I want to take it slow. If it's meant to be, it will be. We need to nurture our relationship and see where it takes us."

"Can I give you a kiss good night?"

I nodded my head, letting him know it was okay. I leaned in for the kiss, his mouth warm and sensual, and I could taste the alcohol on his lips. We pulled apart at the same time.

"Good night, Jessica."

"Good night, Grayson."

I walked up the stairs to my apartment alone that night feeling great. I wanted to see if Grayson was worth the risk of possibly getting hurt again. Only time would tell. I washed my face, brushed my teeth, and put on my nightgown. I read a little of my book before drifting off to sleep, dreaming of my night on the river cruise with Grayson.

CHAPTER 11

*A*fter the river cruise, Grayson and I saw more of each other. The four of us traipsed all over Germany, visiting the wonderful sites, and soon we made our way into neighboring countries. There was just so much to see.

In honor of my birthday, Crystal and company planned a special getaway. Crystal was the chief planner, with Grayson and Charles just going along with what she said. I knew they were planning something, but the details were a secret. I was told to pack a light overnight bag. That was my first clue that we'd be traveling. I was excited and happy that my friends thought enough of me to plan a special birthday trip.

Momma would always make my favorite dinner and bake a chocolate cake for my birthdays. I'd usually have one gift to open, and it was usually a book. I think I was a happy kid, despite my loneliness and my longing for something more. If I knew one thing for sure, I knew my momma loved me. I was thinking more and more about her lately. I'd gotten a few letters, but it took a long time for a letter to get from Texas to Germany. By the time I got the letter, it was old news. I enjoyed reading about her visits to the farmers' market and her trips to the library. She said someone had to keep the library card current now that I wasn't there. She never mentioned my uncle, and that was just as well. I didn't really care what he was up to.

Momma's letters were always happy and, although she didn't write a lot, she made sure she ended every letter with, "Love you and miss you, Momma." I had it on my list to fly back and see her. It seemed something always came up. I was busy doing my job and my charity work while stationed in Africa. My duties at the Amerika Haus kept me busy, but it was the nightlife and traveling with my friends that really kept me busy. I started to feel guilty about not visiting Momma. There was a light rap on my door. I was sure it was Crystal letting me know it was time to go. I opened the door to see Crystal, smiling ear to ear.

"Are you ready to party, birthday girl?" she said as she gave me a little wink.

"I guess. I still don't know where you're taking me. When are you going to tell me?"

"When we get to the train station, and we hand you your ticket!"

"Where are Charles and Grayson?" I asked as I closed the door and started to walk down the steps leading to the sidewalk. "Are they meeting us at the train station?"

"Yes, they had a few loose ends to tie up. Don't worry ... Grayson is coming," she said, laughing.

"I wasn't worried about him coming or not," I said to her, quietly miffed that she'd made that statement.

We walked the couple of blocks to the train station. We were beginning to know that route like the back of our hands. We'd made it a lot, and it was very convenient to be so close to our homes and workplace, too. Sure enough, just as she'd said, they were waiting for us near the ticket booth. As we approached them, Charles and Grayson both had smirks on their faces that told me they were quite pleased about something. As we got closer, I could see that each had their hand in the air, waving something. Charles held out the ticket for Crystal to take, and Grayson gave me mine.

"Paris! We're going to Paris?" I shrieked.

All three of them nodded their heads, and their smiles were enormous and brilliant. I couldn't help but smile, too. Paris. This was going to be a birthday that I'd never forget!

We were too excited to sleep much on the train. We played cards, read, and chatted. It seemed we were always with Crystal and Charles, and having alone time with Grayson was becoming increasingly difficult.

"What was it like growing up in California?" I asked, hoping it would prompt more dialogue.

"It wasn't typical, that's for sure," he said, chuckling.

"Oh? How so?" I asked, trying not to sound like I was digging, but I was curious.

"During the summer, we hung out at the beach from sunup to sundown. I surfed a great deal," he added, grinning.

"A surfer dude!" I said boldly.

He nodded his head and grinned as if recalling the fond memories.

"I've never even seen the Pacific Ocean, except for in books," I volunteered.

"It's pretty awesome. The Pacific coastline is a lot different than the Atlantic," he offered.

I didn't want to tell him and sound like a know-it-all … but I'd seen pictures in books and could tell there was a difference.

When we finally arrived at our destination, it was early evening. We flagged down a cab and soon, were on our way to the hotel. It was in the heart of Paris, and I immediately felt a rush that I hadn't experienced before. Crystal and Charles filled out the guest information cards and checked us in. We rode the elevator to the fourth floor. I guess I just assumed that Crystal and I'd be sharing a room. I was shocked when Charles opened one door, and Crystal followed behind him. Soon Grayson was unlocking what would be our room. I wasn't sure how I felt about it, but I knew we were in Paris, the most romantic city in the world, and I felt well … lured by her ambiance.

The room was on the small side, but the furniture was trendy with a high gloss finish and vibrant colors. A chic disco ball light prominently hung from the ceiling, rounding out the artistic flair Paris was known for. After the two of us had checked out our accommodations for the weekend, we decided to unpack the few items we'd brought, and hang them up. We were just about finished when there was a light tap on our door. I rushed to it and swung it wide open. Standing in the hallway were Charles and Crystal, smooching.

"*Ahem,*" I said, clearing my throat.

"Oh, hey. You and Grayson ready to go paint the town red?" Crystal said, laughing.

I had become fond of Crystal, but sometimes she irritated me. I wasn't sure what exactly she was doing with Charles, but I imagined it was something she'd done a few times before.

Grayson and I followed behind the two lovebirds. We made our way downstairs to the quaint restaurant and bar, where we had a delightful dinner consisting of exquisite cheese and red wine, followed by salad, coq au vin, and finally crème brûlée for dessert. We all agreed we'd never had chicken prepared quite like that before.

After dinner, we walked around downtown, taking in all the sights and sounds of Paris. We found our way to a sidewalk café that served drinks, and although my better senses said I'd had enough, I drank another glass of wine, making it three for the evening. I started getting flirty with Grayson, and before I realized it, we were holding hands, and smiling—a lot! We discussed our game plan for the following day. We were going to get up early, have a light breakfast, and then take in the Eiffel Tower, the Louvre, and a boat ride on the Seine. We paid our tab and walked the few blocks back to the hotel. As we approached our rooms, I realized this meant I had to make a big decision.

"Good night you two," Crystal bellowed.

"Sheesh, Crystal. Keep it down. You're going to wake up the other guests."

"Get a good night's rest. We have a lot of sightseeing to do tomorrow," she said as she shut the door to their room and left us standing there.

Grayson walked over to the door and unlocked it with the key. He pushed it open for me to enter first. After we had entered the room, I realized I wasn't ready for whatever he thought was going to take place.

"Grayson, I don't know what you're expecting, but nothing is going to take place in that bed tonight, besides sleeping."

"Okay, that's fine with me. I didn't really want the rooms to be arranged like this. It was Charles and Crystal's idea. Look, I'll take the bedspread off, roll it up like a bolster and put it down the middle. This side is your half, and this side is mine," he said, showing with his hands the line of division.

"Boy, that is such a relief," I said, reaching out and lightly touching him on the arm to let him know how thoughtful he was being. He smiled.

"If you don't mind, I'll sleep with my clothes on," I said to him.

"Is it okay if I take my pants off? I'll leave everything else on, including my socks; it's just not that comfortable sleeping in jeans," he added bashfully.

"That's fine," I said, smiling again at his thoughtfulness.

We talked for hours, telling each other about our childhoods. He told me how he'd spent hours surfing and hanging out with his friends—his life in California was so different from mine. His family sounded interesting, although he said they were the reason he joined the military and moved away. We had that in common. I didn't want to get away from Momma as much as my circumstances. Grayson said he found himself being too carefree and not taking life seriously enough. After talking with a recruiter one day, he realized he needed to grow up and take some responsibility. His parents couldn't understand why a young man from a well-to-do family would join the military. I admired his courage to serve the nation and for the first time, I felt an overabundance of pride for Grayson and his core values. Soon he drifted off to sleep and I could hear him softly breathing, laying inches from me.

I lay awake for a long time, wondering how many times he'd slept in a bed with a woman and resisted the sexual urgency to fulfill his pent-up desires. I wondered how many women slept in a bed with a gorgeous man and resisted the urge to succumb to his every demand

—or her demand for that matter. It was no use. I wasn't that woman, and he wasn't that man. Paris. This was why I hadn't wanted to come to Paris. It had a romantic implication just in its name. I wondered if Josh ever made it to Paris. Finally realizing that worrying about Josh, Grayson, or even Paris, was not getting me the much-needed sleep I'd require for a full day of sightseeing, I finally drifted off to sleep.

I awoke the next morning feeling a body up close to me, an arm swung over my shoulder, a leg lying across mine, and warm breaths softly blowing my hair! I thought I was dreaming, but soon realized it was Grayson snuggling up against my body. Thank God I had my clothes on. Then I remembered he was only half-dressed. I quietly took his arm off my shoulder and let it fall gently on the bed. I wiggled myself out from under his leg and quietly got out of bed. There on the floor was the homemade bolster he unwaveringly convinced me would work. Disgusted with thinking some rolled-up bedspread would keep us separated, I gathered my clean clothes and locked myself in the bathroom to shower and get ready for our hectic day of sightseeing.

When I came out of the bathroom, Grayson was up and dressed.

"Good morning. Did you sleep well?" he asked with his back turned—smirking, I gathered, because of what had happened.

"Actually, no, I didn't," I said smugly.

"I slept like a baby. It was either the alcohol or …"

"Or, maybe it was all the snuggling we did last night!" I bellowed.

"Snuggling? We snuggled?" he asked, surprised.

"Don't give me that innocent look, or tone, Grayson. You know exactly what took place here last night. That … that … homemade divider thing you made, rolled out of bed, or maybe it was thrown out, who knows, and you were curled up against me with your leg thrown over mine!"

Grayson started laughing at me. That upset me more. I pointed my finger at him to let him know I really meant it. Shaking my finger at him, I said, "I trusted you."

"Hold on a minute, Jessica. Nothing happened. So we cuddled a little bit. You had your clothes on, and I basically had mine on. Calm down. Don't let this upset you so much." With that, he gathered his things and went into the bathroom to shower and get ready, leaving me in the room to stew some more. I'd eventually get over it. He had a point. Nothing had happened. When he came back out of the bathroom, I coyly smiled and winked letting him know all was forgiven.

After breakfast, the four of us continued with our travel itinerary. Next stop—the Eiffel Tower.

I was in awe of its splendor and the size of it. We took many pictures from every angle so that we could capture the sheer grandeur of the tower. It was so surreal; I'd never seen anything like it before. We were snapping pictures of each other when another tourist came over and asked if we'd like a picture taken of the four of us together. We posed under the arches, Charles with his arm around Crystal, and Grayson with his around me—just four young people having the time of their lives in Paris.

Our next stop was the Louvre. The size of the Louvre was impressive. I thought I'd be the only one interested in the paintings, but Grayson expressed a liking for them as well. I was excited beyond words when we came across Leonardo da Vinci's *Mona Lisa*, protected in its glass case. I'd seen it in books before, but seeing it in person took my breath away. I had the same jittery feeling when we came across Michelangelo's *Slaves*. It was unreal being in the same room with these beautiful works of art. Being in Paris was crazy enough, but seeing the Eiffel Tower, and now the Louvre, was testimony that we were indeed in Paris! We walked the hallways, looking at the various paintings for about an hour. It was extremely crowded inside, and Crystal and Charles said they needed some air. As much as I didn't want to leave, the crowd was getting to me as well. We found a grassy area near the museum and plotted out our next course.

After we rested a while and talked about what we'd seen so far, we decided we'd better get a move on to see the rest. We'd be here for such a short time. We headed to the Arc de Triomphe monument and took some more pictures. Crystal and I were clowning around, hugging each other while Grayson snapped the shots. Charles and Grayson were fooling around, too, and we got some pictures of them acting playful. Crystal wanted her picture taken with Charles, so I obliged by taking a few different poses.

"Don't you want your picture taken with Grayson?" she teased.

Grayson and I humored Crystal with her request, smiling and making the best of another awkward situation. After the picture taking, we headed over to the Champs-Elysées, where we found a cute café for a late lunch. After we had eaten, we walked around and looked at all the specialty shops, drooling over the merchandise, and shocked by the prices, even if they were in francs.

I don't know why, but Momma popped into my head. I guess it was looking at all the lovely merchandise in the windows. I wonder if she wore the scarf I bought her from Africa or wore the Birkenstock shoes from Germany that cost me a pretty penny. I wondered what I could get Momma from Paris that would be special. Just as I was contemplating a gift idea, we came across a perfume shop. I convinced Crystal to go in with me. I was relieved to hear the sales clerk speak English. She helped me find a nice floral scent that would be perfect for Momma.

After a lovely night and day in Paris, it was time to take the train home. We boarded an evening train and, exhausted from all the walking and sightseeing, we slept the entire way back to Frankfurt.

The conductor walked down the aisle, letting us know that we were arriving in Frankfurt and to prepare to disembark. We gathered our belongings, awaiting final word that we had arrived. I looked out the window, and all I could see was darkness—until we approached the well-lit train station.

"I'm exhausted, but in a good way," Crystal said, pausing and then hugging Charles.

"It was the best birthday present. I was so surprised!"

We walked the short distance to our houses, with Charles and Grayson in tow. They wanted to make sure we got home safely, and I appreciated their thoughtfulness. I wasn't convinced if Charles was being thoughtful, or hoping for an invitation to spend the night with Crystal. Either way, I felt deep down in my heart that Grayson was, and that's all that really mattered.

"Well, here we are, home at last." I said. "Tomorrow will come soon enough. Work, ugh!" I added.

I looked over to say good night one last time and witnessed Charles and Crystal tightly intertwined, kissing, and laughing. I felt like I was invading their privacy. Irritated once again with her behavior, I cleared my throat.

"*Ahem*, Crystal! Get a room," I said.

She retorted, "I did, in Paris!" We both laughed.

They broke up their little fraternization and came over to join us.

"Sorry about that," she said amusedly.

I gave her a smirk that let her know she was annoying me. It was getting late, and I wanted to call it a night. "Thanks, everyone. Have a great evening. See you around, Grayson … Charles. See you tomorrow, Crystal."

Everyone smiled at me and comments were flying out of their mouths such as, yes it was fun, we must do it again, and the like. I walked up the stairs, put the key in the door, and once inside, let out a sigh of relief that although it truly was the best birthday ever, I was so glad it was over!

CHAPTER 12

J had been thinking about Momma and Texas a lot lately. I decided I'd make a trip back home. I had about fifteen months left on my assignment in Germany, and part of the benefits of working for the government and living overseas was a trip home every three years. I hadn't taken it while I was in Africa, mainly because I was so busy with all the charities and then there was Andrew, too. But that was all behind me now, and except for Crystal, Grayson, and Charles, I was not tied down, and I had plenty of leave saved up for the trip to the United States.

I told Crystal I was going on a vacation, back to Texas to see Momma. She seemed surprised.

"I didn't realize you were planning on a trip to Texas," she said searching for more details. "Is everything okay? You didn't receive any bad news did you?" she added, showing me she cared. Or was it just to meet some criteria for acting as if she cared? I still hadn't figured out where we stood with our friendship. She was so different from Lauren and Birdie.

"Everything is fine," I said matter-of-factly, although I wasn't absolutely sure, as Momma's letters were generic and vague at best.

"How long will you be gone?"

"About three weeks," I said, smiling, finally realizing I was happy about going home.

"Did you tell Grayson?"

"No ... I wasn't aware I had to let him know," I retorted.

Crystal gave me a look that said she disapproved of my firm stance, shrugged her shoulders and went looking for someone else in the office she could attach herself to. She was like that. Couldn't stand to be alone, and the mere thought of me being away for three weeks already had her agitated and filled with anxiety. I, on the other hand, liked being alone sometimes. I enjoyed reading a good book, or sitting in a quiet room with a view and letting my mind take me places. I learned early on that if you can't be your own best company, you'll not be good company for others. Crystal had not learned that lesson yet. She had to be the life of the party, the center of attention, and I was beginning to see that she didn't feel complete without some man in her life—any man.

I thought about what Crystal had said—regarding my telling Grayson about my travel plans. The more I thought about it, the more I concluded I should. After all, he was my friend. I wasn't sure if it was the guilt or the obligation I felt like his friend, but nevertheless, I decided I'd inform him of my decision the next time I saw him.

The next few days were odd. Crystal seemed aloof—as if she was trying to distance herself from me. I wasn't sure what that was about, but I assumed it was some mechanism she developed when she felt anxious. It was clear to me that she wasn't sure what she was going to do while I was away.

I had an idea that she'd run into the arms of Charles on most nights, but she'd have to get a new office friend during the daytime while I was gone. I noticed she was spending more time at the desk of one of our co-workers. If it was supposed to bother me, it didn't. I was glad for the break, actually. Each night after work, she had some excuse to stay behind, leaving me to walk home alone.

It began to bother me a little that she could switch off our friendship so casually, but then again, she was unique, and one thing I'd learned was that you can't change people. You have to either accept them for who they are, or move on. As my departure date loomed, I still had not had the opportunity to let Grayson know. I looked up his office number on the Garrison directory and placed a call to him.

"Hi, Grayson. It's me, Jessica. How are you?"

"I'm good. I haven't heard from you in a while. Is everything okay?" he added sincerely.

"I'm really good," I replied cheerfully. "Listen, the reason I'm calling … I'm getting ready to go back to Texas for a little R & R, and visit my momma. I'll be gone for three weeks," I added quickly before he could ask me anything.

After a few seconds of silence, he said, "Oh, okay. That's good," he replied. Obviously, I had taken him by surprise, and he was trying not to disclose his bewilderment. He then added, "I'll miss you."

Now who was shocked and surprised? What could I say to that? I cleared my throat and I guess he could tell it put me in an awkward situation, so before I could answer him, he quickly added, "We'll get together when you return. I have to get back to work. Have a safe trip."

THE DAY COULDN'T COME SOON ENOUGH for me to board that plane bound for Texas! I had a lot to think about as the hours passed, flying high up in the atmosphere—comingling with the clouds and air, and all the other elements of earth and heaven. I thought about how my life had evolved, growing up poor in a little town, graduating from the State Department as a specialist, and now traveling the world. Some would say I was living the American dream. I guess I was. It just hadn't played out like I thought it would. I guess life never does. Momma used to tell me, "It's not what you're dealt, but how you play your hand." I tried to remember that.

The flight was long, but not as long as when I flew to Africa. I landed in New York, and then took a plane to Atlanta. From Georgia, I flew into the airport nearest my house and took a cab the rest of the way in. It was late when the taxi pulled up in front of the house with the peeling paint, the broken railings on the porch, and the overgrown vegetation. I never realized how shabby the house was when I lived there. It really needed some TLC. I thought about Andrew, and how he could really fix up the house.

Deep inside, I wondered if everything was okay with Momma. I paid the cab driver, got my bag, and walked up the dirt path that led to the porch. I could see the glow of lights in the house, so I assumed she was still awake. I didn't want to startle her, but I knew the hour was late, so I knocked lightly, turning the knob to the door at the same time. It was unlocked.

"Momma? Momma, it's me, Jessica. I'm home."

I slowly opened the door wider and let myself in. I heard rustling coming from the back room. Out came Momma with her rifle!

"Momma, it's just me, Jessica!"

"Child! You scared me."

Momma put the gun down and came running toward me. She hugged me tightly, trying to make up for our separation these last five years. Tears were running down her face like water coming out of a faucet.

"Come sit down," she said as she made her way into the kitchen. "Are you hungry?"

"No. I ate on the plane. I'm more tired than hungry, Momma. It was a long flight." Seeing the hurt on her face, I suddenly regretted telling her I was tired. But, being the great momma that she was, she said, "We can get caught up in the morning."

My room hadn't changed a bit. Momma had kept everything the same. I looked at the old, faded posters on my walls, the knickknacks I'd collected and displayed on my dresser, and of course, all my books. One entire wall was lined with bookshelves, each one loaded with books. I picked one from the shelf and blew the dust off the cover. I slowly leafed through the pages. It was a travel book with colorful photos of faraway places. I sighed. It didn't seem that long ago that Josh and I had sat on the porch, dreaming of these places. I wondered how he was, and what he'd been up to. I bet he was married and had children, too.

I unpacked a nightgown, went to the one bathroom in our tiny house, washed my face, and brushed my teeth. I looked around the small, dark bathroom. It wasn't much to see, but the old house gave me comfort, and I was glad to be back. I knew that, as tired as I was, sleep wouldn't come easily since I had jet lag. I looked at another book or two and finally nodded off sometime late into the night. Once I was asleep, I slept hard, only to awaken at the soft rap on my door, and Momma urging me to get up.

"Hey, sleepyhead, are you going to sleep your day away?" she light-heartedly inquired.

"What time is it?" I responded in between yawns.

"Ten thirty."

"Ten thirty!" I exclaimed. "Give me a few minutes. I'm getting right up."

I pulled myself together, and after several minutes of water rushing over my face and head, I was awake. I dressed and wandered out to the kitchen, where I could smell the wonderful aromas of coffee brewing and bacon frying. It was great to be home.

"Good morning. Coffee?" Momma asked me cheerfully.

"Yes, please."

"What else are you making?" I asked in between sips of the strong, but delicious coffee.

"Scrambled eggs, is that okay?"

"Anything sounds great about now. I'm hungry!"

After the small talk about breakfast, Momma asked me about the job, friends, and Josh—in that order. As I was answering her first two questions, I was trying to decide how to handle the latter.

"I love my job! It's everything I dreamt it would be, and more," I said, smiling so hard I thought my face would crack.

Momma was flipping the bacon, and the spattering of the grease was the only sound for a moment. I watched her as she placed a paper towel on a plate to drain the bacon, soaking most of the grease. She methodically opened the refrigerator and took out the eggs. One by one, she cracked eggs into a bowl. Whipping them just till they frothed, she poured them into the pan that she'd cooked the bacon in.

The eggs sizzled in the remaining grease, and the aroma of bacon and eggs filled the kitchen.

We ate in silence for a few minutes. In between bites I told her how good everything tasted.

"Have you made a lot of friends, Jessica?"

"I've met some. You know me, Momma. I choose my friends cautiously, but the ones I have, well … they are priceless," I said smiling. "Now, take Birdie."

Momma quickly shot me a look. "Birdie? What in the heck kind of name is that?"

"Her real name is Roberta. Her family and friends call her Birdie. It was kind of like we were meant to be friends. Her nickname is Birdie, and the kids used to call me Owl," I said through clenched teeth.

"You didn't let her call you Owl, did you?"

"No. We settled on Jessica," I said, laughing at Momma's disgusted tone and look at the thought of her only daughter being called Owl.

"My friend in Germany is Crystal. She was born and raised in Germany."

"Does she speak English?" Momma asked me with a surprised look on her face.

"Yes, Momma, she speaks English."

I knew Momma was itching to ask me about Josh and any other guy, so I decided to beat her to the punch.

"I haven't seen Josh since we left D.C."

"What happened?" she asked me with a look of concern.

I don't normally like to lie to Momma, but the less she knew about the breakup, the better.

"It was mutual, Momma. He was moving clear around the world, the opposite side of where I was going. It was going to be too difficult continuing with a relationship with that much distance between us." Sensing that Momma didn't buy the explanation, I added, "We're still friends."

Momma got up from the table, took our plates to the sink, and began to fill up it with warm, soapy water. I knew she was thinking too deeply about Josh and me. To get her mind off the mutual breakup, I mentioned Andrew.

"I did meet a nice fellow in Africa."

Momma dried her hands on her apron and slowly turned around to face me at the table.

"What is his name?"

"Andrew. He is a missionary, and Momma, he does a lot of wonderful things for the people in Africa. His group builds churches and schools," I said proudly.

"What happened?"

"You mean, what happened between us?"

Momma nodded her head.

"It just wasn't the right time for Andrew, Momma. He was very involved, and rightly so, with his charitable work. He wasn't going to give that up, and I wouldn't have expected him to. Besides, I got my orders to go to Germany, and I had to leave Birdie, Bitalo, and Andrew behind," I said gloomily, feeling the effects of leaving my friends behind for the first time in a long time. I shook off the sadness and decided to tell Momma about Grayson.

"I have a new friend. His name is Grayson. He's in the U. S. Army," I added.

Momma made some grunting noise, and I wasn't sure if it was because I mentioned I had a new friend or the fact he was in the service. It didn't really matter, as Grayson and I were only friends, and wouldn't be anything more. There was no need to tell Momma too much. She'd never be meeting him.

Momma finished the dishes.

"Would you care for a second cup of coffee?"

"I don't mind if I do," I said, getting up and heading to the coffee pot.

"While you finish up your coffee, I'm going to freshen up a bit. What do you want to do today?"

"I hadn't really thought too hard about it. I mainly want to be with you, Momma."

"Let's go into town. We can go to the library, and I need to pick up a few items at the grocery store for dinner."

Momma made no mention of my uncle, and I wasn't about to. I was fine with him staying down at his house. I hoped he wouldn't ruin my visit.

Momma and I had a wonderful time catching up and just being together. We made cookies, took long walks, and when we visited the library, the same librarian was still there! She asked me if I'd seen Lauren and Josh lately. I smiled and said no. It was somewhat ironic, that the same little town I couldn't wait to get away from was making me feel warm inside—making me smile, making me happy. Thinking back, it really wasn't that awful growing up there. Uncle made it feel bad, but if it weren't for Momma and my friends, I'd have been a very unhappy child. I had many fond memories of riding bikes, visiting the library, and throwing stones in the creek. It wasn't all bad, that's for sure.

My visit was soon over, and I had to head back to Germany. I knew Momma was anticipating it before the day even came. I was having such a nice time reconnecting with her, that I didn't see the day approaching until it was upon me. On my last night, Momma made my favorite dinner: fried chicken, mashed potatoes, and corn on the cob, with blueberry cobbler for dessert. I enjoyed every bit as if it were the last time I'd ever taste her cooking.

"Momma, this is delicious! I'm savoring each bite."

Momma laughed. "Don't the Germans know how to fry chicken?"

"They make some delicious chicken and veal dishes, but it's not like this," I added, taking another bite off the chicken leg I held in my hand.

I was dreading the tears we'd both shed on the morning of my departure. Momma didn't disappoint me. She cried softly as she hugged me.

"Don't wait so long till you come back," she scowled.

"I won't, Momma. I promise."

The taxi ride to the airport was a somber one. I already missed Momma. The flight was uneventful, and several hours later, I was picking up my luggage at baggage claim at the airport in Frankfurt. I took an extra day of leave so that I could get over the jet lag. I wasn't sure what I was feeling, but I almost regretted being back. I think living in foreign and exotic places was getting to me. I longed for a simpler life, and it was time for me to go stateside. I had about thirteen months left on my tour. It was time for rotation.

I didn't know what was available in the States, but I was hoping maybe I could be assigned somewhere in Texas so I could be close to Momma. She hadn't said that she'd been ill, but she did look a little tired and thinner than I recalled. She was probably being run ragged taking care of my stupid uncle. I made a mental note to check with personnel and see if I could put down some stateside assignment choices. Meanwhile, I'd put all my energy into Amerika Haus, and soon the time would come for me to move on. Of course, even the best-laid plans can get a kink in them.

Crystal was happy to see me. She gave me a hug that about took my breath away.

"I really missed you, Jessica!" she said in her heavy accent.

I didn't want to lie, but I didn't want to hurt her feelings either, so I nodded, and said, "I missed you, too."

I guess I did miss her; I wasn't sure. I knew I'd have a lot of work to catch up on, so I told her we'd get caught up later.

"Let me wade through this in-box, and see what important matters I need to take care of."

Most of the day I was busy doing just that, wading through mounds of paper, and trying to follow up on all my important messages. I worked through lunch, even. Soon the clock said five o'clock and it was time to go home. Crystal and I made small talk as we made our way to our respective homes. I didn't mention Grayson, and she didn't say a word about Charles. I found that a bit odd, but went with it, as I didn't really want to discuss them right now, anyway.

"Boy, am I going to sleep like a baby," I said, walking slowly up the stairs to my door.

"You were busy all day. You didn't even have enough time for me," she said, pouting.

"Auf Wiedersehen, Crystal."

"Auf Wiedersehen, Jessica."

~

A COUPLE of weeks went by and before I knew it, Crystal and I were back in our old pattern. We met Charles and Grayson at the local pub, and soon we were back in the routine we'd had before I went to visit Momma. I enjoyed the music, and I enjoyed the group's company. It was better than sitting home alone night after night. I found myself laughing at Grayson's jokes more, and I found myself letting him hold my hand more often. I didn't want to think I couldn't exist without him, or any guy for that matter. I didn't want to give off the impression that I needed a man in order to be happy—not like Crystal. But … I did start to feel something for Grayson, and it was after one of the fun nights at the corner pub that I let my guard down, and let him kiss me again.

We were walking home, and he stopped dead in his tracks and pulled me close. I could feel the warmth of his breath. I admit I was slightly aroused by his take-charge attitude. Moments later, we were kissing. His lips were warm and gentle, softly kissing me while holding my head. He ran his free hand through my hair, and it sent chills up my spine and down my arms. After a few moments, we parted.

Not knowing what to say or how to act, we both just stood only inches apart. I was still feeling somewhat lightheaded from the kiss, or maybe it was the beer or a combination of both. He pulled me close once again, but only for a hug. I pulled away so I could tell him what I was feeling. I wasn't sure what I was going to say.

"Grayson, I don't know if that was the right thing to do."

"What do you mean, Jessica?"

"Taking this … whatever this is between us, to the next level."

"I'm sorry if I pushed myself on you," he said, hanging his head in shame.

Pulling his head up so I could look him straight in the eyes, I said, "There is no shame in how you feel about me, or how I feel about you. What I'm concerned about, and I know you have to be thinking this, too, is that you're in the Army and I'm assigned to the State Department, and I'm only here for thirteen more months, then I'll be gone …"

"I know, Jessica. I know."

We held hands and started walking toward my house. I wanted to tell him about Josh, and about Andrew, but I was afraid to. I didn't want him to think I was a big baby. I just didn't want to get hurt again.

"Let's just take it slowly, Grayson. It's too hard to have a long-distance relationship."

"I've never met anyone quite like you. Most girls over here are trying to get married."

Laughing, but realizing the seriousness of our discussion, I said, "Trust me, I *am* the marrying kind. I just don't do well bouncing from guy to guy. But, I'm also not a prude. What I'd do to jump your bones right now!" I said, squeezing him close. "I just don't want too many regrets. I have had a few already in my short life." I was beginning to care for him more than I could've imagined. It unnerved me.

We approached the walk that would lead to my door, stopping for a second and seizing the moment for one last kiss. I pulled away from his warm lips, smiled, and walked up the stairs to my door. Looking back one last time, I saw Grayson walking away, and once again, I felt alone.

CHAPTER 13

J tried to put work ahead of Grayson, but I was more aware
of my feelings and this intensified my fear of losing him.
Over the next several days, I threw myself into my work, promoting
an event on behalf of Amerika Haus. It took up a lot of my time, and
that was a good thing. I had a host of items I needed to attend to,
including designing and ordering flyers, choosing appetizers carefully
and having invitations sent to commanding officers in the local area
as well as local dignitaries. I was grateful that Grayson understood my
commitment to Amerika Haus and not a bit surprised that he offered
to help by licking the many envelopes I'd send through the embassy's
postal system.

"How many invitations are here?" Grayson asked as he drew out
another handful, getting ready to lick away.

"About fifty," I responded, gathering a few myself.

"I have an idea," he said, bolting up out of the chair and opening
my kitchen cabinet.

"What are you looking for?"

"I found it," he said, coming back to the table with a small bowl full
of water and a sponge.

"This is much better than licking," he said as he dipped the corner of the sponge into the water and swiped it across the strip of glue on the envelope flap.

"How'd you get to be so smart, surfer boy?" I asked, laughing.

"Surfer Boy—is that my new nickname?"

I nodded. I don't know why I called him that. I'd never called him that before. I knew he used to surf out in California, but truthfully, I didn't see him in that role any more than he probably did.

"I'll have to come up with a nickname for you," he responded jovially.

"I already have a nickname—Owl," I admitted begrudgingly.

"Owl? How'd you get that name?"

"The kids at school thought my eyes looked like owl eyes. I was upset at first but after further investigation, I discovered that owls are pretty fascinating creatures. I see it more as a compliment, really."

I decided to share the story about Roberta. "My roommate in Africa's real name was Roberta, but her friends and family called her Birdie. I didn't think it would go over very well with Birdie and Owl sharing a room so we decided on Birdie for her and Jessica for me."

We both erupted in laughter.

"Stop! You're making my side hurt, Grayson," I said, poking him in the ribs.

We finished sealing all the invitations in record time, despite the laughter and joking we did. It was getting late and I knew Grayson would have to get up at dawn to participate in the physical training the Army required him to do. He gathered his things and headed for the door. He placed his hand on the doorknob and started to turn it. He stopped and turned toward me.

"Jessica, have you thought any more about us?"

Shaking my head that I hadn't given it too much thought, I quickly added, "I've been so preoccupied with this big event. I've not thought about much of anything besides this …" I admitted, trailing off and looking down at the ground, knowing that wasn't exactly what he wanted to hear. I hated to lie to him, but I wasn't ready to confront what I was beginning to feel.

He nodded his head that he understood. We were standing fairly close to one another and the heat I could feel from his body radiated throughout my being. He reached for my arms and pulled me even closer and soon we were kissing. His kisses were soft and sweet—nothing wet or sloppy. He was a pure gentleman in every sense of the word. Our relationship was complicated, though. He was in the military, and I was a civil servant—either one of us could be transferred at any moment.

After Grayson had left, I began to clean up the area where we'd been inserting and sealing invitations. I was really starting to care for him, but something was causing me not to surrender my heart and open my arms to him. I didn't want to admit that it could be Josh that was keeping Grayson more than an arm's length from me. I'd told myself a long time ago that I was over him. I didn't think about him at all, but the true test was when we all went to Paris. I needed closure. I decided to locate Josh.

I KNEW it couldn't be that difficult to locate him. He was, after all, a civil servant with the State Department as I was. Although our computer equipment was antiquated compared to today's standards, I was able to look through a huge database that served as a locator for the civilians. Thankfully, it was in alphabetical order and I soon found Josh's name. I had never been even slightly curious where he was before now. Roberta, Bitalo, and Andrew had occupied my time while in Africa, and now Grayson in Germany. I had to find out if he was single, or engaged, married, with or without children. I had to know if life had been kind to him. I don't know why I felt I had to know these things, but I did. I never really understood what had happened to us back in D.C. Maybe now he'd tell me.

I located his name and looked at the screen, reading the various entries by it. He'd been promoted—that was splendid, there was an APO address and unit assignment, and then in the last category the missing piece to the puzzle—where he was assigned. I looked at the word as if it were foreign. I looked at each letter front and backward. I felt my face turn red, and I could feel the heat build in my body. Finally, whispering the word so no one else could hear me, I heard myself say the word—France. I wondered if he had been there all along, or if this was a new assignment. I tried to see if there was any other information regarding his assignment on this locator database, but nothing. I quietly muttered, "I'll be damned. He's in France." I picked up the phone and dialed the number next to his name. After several rings, a female voice identified herself and the department in which she worked. I asked for Josh. My palms were sweaty; my heart was racing a mile a minute. My mouth was so dry my tongue was sticking to the roof of my mouth. I gulped and wetted my lips in the hopes that I wouldn't sound like a frog when I spoke. After about thirty seconds, a male voice came on the line that I didn't recognize, but it'd been years since we'd last spoken.

"This is Josh, can I help you?"

I didn't speak a word. I froze. I tried to make the words come out, but they wouldn't. They just hung in midair like a parachute falling out of the sky.

"Hello? This is Josh. Is anyone on the line?"

I knew I had to say something, so after what seemed like minutes, I uttered my first words. "Josh. This is Jessica."

The silence on the other end of the receiver was unnerving. It made my skin crawl. I wasn't sure if it was because I was expecting him to shout into the receiver *where the heck have you been*, or *I've missed you so much*, or well … you get the picture. Unfortunately, none of those things came out of his mouth—just silence.

One of us had to take the next step, and I guessed it was going to be me. I gathered all my strength deep down inside and I said the following to him. "I know it's been ages … I've thought about you a lot. How have you been?" I said, trying hard to control my emotions and not let him hear my voice crack.

"I've been good," he said, sounding a little annoyed.

"Listen, I don't mean to barge in on you, especially after all this time. I just wanted to know what you'd been up to—we were friends once, you know," I said matter-of-factly.

I wanted to jump down his throat and yell at him—ask him why he'd treated me so rotten in D.C., and why he left so many things unanswered for me. Instead, I asked him how he'd been, and other small talk. I guess it just wasn't worth the argument. To my surprise, he started telling me that he was doing pretty well. I guess the iceberg began to melt. He opened up more, and as the conversation continued, he told me that he'd been assigned to Turkey and France twice. He said the first time he was in Paris, and now he was in a smaller city, Metz. At first, I didn't catch it, or maybe I just didn't want to. By the third time when he used the pronoun *we*, I realized he had a partner.

"You said 'we.' Are you married?" I asked him, wanting to know the truth so I could move forward with my life.

"Yes. We got married in Paris three years ago. She's from there," he added timidly.

"Congratulations, Josh. That's wonderful news. I'm still single, but I have a boyfriend I really care about. He's in the military—an officer in the Army," I added, showing how proud I was of Grayson's accomplishments.

"Good. Glad to hear you're happy. We're expecting our first child in three months. Marie and I are overwhelmed, but excited beyond words."

I tried to process everything he told me. It was a lot to hear in the first three minutes of a phone conversation, especially with someone you'd not spoken with in over five years.

Realizing I had to make mention of the baby, I congratulated him. "How exciting, Josh. Do you know what you're having?"

I could hear the grin on his face as he responded, "Yes, a girl!"

Now that we'd caught up on the last few years of our life, and were feeling a bit more comfortable, I went for the jugular. I asked him the question that had been plaguing me for years. "Josh, I just have a question for you that I need you to answer. I've been wondering for the last few years why you treated me so badly in the cafeteria that day. I need closure," I added, feeling vulnerable but requiring the answer just the same.

"Oh, Jessica. I'd hoped that you weren't holding on to that. I was a dumb young male trying to show off for my new friends, and I let it get the best of me. I was hoping we'd make up somewhere down the road, and I even secretly hoped we'd get an assignment together. Then, time got in the way, and I met Marie. I felt bad for the way I treated you, but I can't go back in time to fix it. Just know, you were my friend, and I always hoped that if we didn't find our way back together, you'd find someone worthy of your love and friendship."

It took me a few seconds to process what he told me. I was elated that he didn't hate me, or find me repulsive, but at the same time disappointed that he didn't try harder to find me. I guess he was letting me down gently, but I wasn't born yesterday. At least, I knew the truth now. He didn't hate me—he just found someone more to his liking.

"I'm glad you found your life partner, Josh. And, you're going to be a dad!" I said, trying to sound happy for him. "I think you'll make a great dad," I added.

We ended our conversation on a high note and promised to keep in touch. I didn't really think we would, but running into each other in our line of work, or even back home could happen. I hung up the phone not feeling sad, but instead feeling happy—alive. I got the closure I needed, allowing me to move on. I couldn't wait to see Grayson.

CHAPTER 14

I mulled over all the ways to let Grayson know I was in one hundred percent committed to making our relationship develop. Fleeting thoughts of job transfers and the possibility of rejection entered my mind, confusing me even more. It was times like these that I wished Crystal and I were better friends. The little bit of unity we did have had fallen apart over time. I summed up our relationship as a friendship of convenience. She wanted to be busy all the time, and I needed a diversion. Our relationship appeared solid on the outside, but truthfully, I always felt lonely when I was with her.

It was perfect timing when I got the call from Birdie that she and Bitalo were coming to Germany. Apparently they were coming for training. I was excited about seeing them both. Birdie would make sense of my uneasiness regarding Grayson.

I couldn't wait for quitting time. I secretly hoped Grayson would be at our regular waiting place; a bench located on a grassy area near my office building. My heart raced just thinking about him. I had butterflies flitting and fluttering in my stomach, and the palms of my hands were moist—my anxiety level extremely high. I went over every possible scenario in my head of what I'd say to him if I ran into him. I didn't want to sound eager or desperate. I walked the path I normally took, hoping I'd run into him, but as I rounded the corner and came upon our bench, I could see that it was empty. Seeing this as yet another sign we were not meant to be together, I sighed and continued on my way.

IT WAS BEGINNING to get cooler earlier in the evening. Fall was definitely in the air. Soon it would be time for Oktoberfest, a huge festival the Germans put on every year in every part of their country. The traditional holidays would soon be after that. *Holidays. Bah humbug,* I thought to myself. *Who wants to spend the holidays alone?* The only good thing about it was that Birdie and Bitalo would be here, too.

I didn't hear from or see Grayson for several days. I could've called him, but it just gave me more time to think. I buried myself in work. The Amerika Haus was having another huge event—a holiday open house. I was in charge of coordinating it since I'd done such a great job with the other events.

It was a Friday evening, and like most every other night, I took the path past all the buildings, traveling near the small park bench that would lead outside the gates of the embassy. This time, as I rounded the corner, I saw an individual sitting on the bench and as I got closer, I could tell by the outline of this person's body that it was Grayson. I could feel my heart pounding so hard, it felt like it would explode outside the wall of my chest. I found myself grinning ear to ear. I picked up my pace slightly, and soon I was standing in front of him, gazing into his eyes.

"Hello," I said, beaming.

"Hi, long time no see," he said casually.

"I've been meaning to contact you," I said, knowing that was only partially true.

"I've been in the field playing war games," he said, standing up, ready to walk with me.

We walked for about ten minutes, making small talk, as I contemplated what I'd say. I had really missed him, and the idea of him walking so close to me stirred up feelings I had restrained for a very long time. I was just getting up the courage to discuss our relationship when he turned to say something and we both started talking at the very same moment. Laughing at ourselves over the timing, I motioned for him to go first.

"I was wondering if you'd like to go to any of the Oktoberfest festivities with me next week. There's a whole itinerary of events that sound fun. They go all out for beer and wurst here," he added, chuckling.

I already knew a little bit about Oktoberfest from the many books I'd read on customs and traditions from around the world. The big celebration took place in Munich, but every town and small village in Germany celebrated. Frankfurt, being one of the largest cities in Germany, would no doubt party in style. I liked the idea of going with him, and nodded my head, adding, "Sounds fun. I wanted to tell you that Birdie and Bitalo—my dear friends from Africa, will be here for training. I was hoping you wouldn't mind if they came along. They've never been to Germany let alone Oktoberfest." I said.

"The more, the merrier. Besides, as much as you've talked about them, I'm happy to finally meet them," he said, taking my hand.

We were soon in front of the steps that led to my door. We stood facing one another, neither one of us sure what to say or do next.

Reaching for my hands, he looked deeply into my eyes. "I missed you, Jessica," he said lovingly.

I squeezed his hand, acknowledging his statement and letting him know I felt the same. I felt a connection with his touch that transferred throughout my body and soul. At a loss for words, and not wanting to say something that required further explanation, I quickly said, "It's getting late. I have a lot of homework to do regarding the holiday open house for Amerika Haus."

Before he could kiss me, I pulled my hands loose from his hold and started to walk up the steps.

"Good night, Jessica," he called out to me.

"Good night, Grayson," I said softly.

CHAPTER 15

$\mathcal{I}$ was excited to see Birdie and Bitalo, and I also let Crystal know they were coming. We made arrangements to meet at the hotel near the embassy compound, where they'd be staying during their training. I arrived a bit early in anticipation of seeing them.

I saw them from a distance as they made their way to the reservation desk. I couldn't contain my excitement and rushed to greet them.

Hugging Birdie first and then Bitalo, I said to them, "I'm so happy to see you two."

"You look great, Jessica," Birdie said. Bitalo nodded.

Birdie and Bitalo checked in as I waited. Getting their keys to their respective rooms, we started walking toward the elevator that would take us to their floor.

"I hope you're in the partying mood. It's Oktoberfest time here in Germany," I said, smiling.

"I know! I looked up some stuff about Germany, and it was highlighted in all of the literature. Beer, bratwurst, and lederhosen." Turning toward Bitalo, Birdie asked him, "Did you remember to pack your lederhosen?"

Bitalo gently and lovingly gave her shoulder a little shove.

We reached their rooms and I followed behind Birdie as she unlocked and entered her room.

"These are pretty nice accommodations," she said, surprised but happy.

"How are you?" I asked her since we were alone, and could talk openly.

"Great. Things are fantastic—both in Uganda and with Bitalo!" she said in a very upbeat tone.

"I'm so happy for you both. I have a little bit of news to share with you as well."

I told her all about Grayson. She was all ears. When I was finished, she informed me that from time to time she ran into Andrew. She also told me that he was aware that she'd be seeing me, and passed on that he wished me well.

"I'm glad he's doing well," I said softly. "I can't wait for you to meet Grayson. He's such a special guy. I just don't really know where we are in our relationship. I get the impression he'd like to be more than friends, but I'm scared to commit," I told her as she unpacked her items and hung them in the closet.

"Well, Jessica. You have commitment phobia, and rightly so. I'm here to tell you … just do what comes naturally."

We made arrangements to get together for dinner during the next few days and discuss our Oktoberfest plans.

JUST AS I HAD SUSPECTED, Frankfurt went all out for the yearly celebration. At the last moment, I asked Crystal and her latest beau if they wanted to go with us. Her relationship with Charles had fizzled out. I figured a celebration as grand as Oktoberfest would be much more fun with a group. One thing led to another and soon there were several of us going in one large group. The word got around in my office that we were going, and Grayson had some buddies who wanted to go as well. Unfortunately, Charles wanted to go, too. I thought it would be awkward but Charles was a good-looking guy, and soon he had not just one pretty girl on his arm, but two. He wasn't even thinking about poor old Crystal—not even for a minute.

Grayson and I were meeting Birdie and Bitalo at their hotel. I was a little nervous, hoping the three of them would hit it off. The fear was unwarranted as they more than hit it off. Soon Bitalo and Grayson were talking up a storm, and Birdie and I beamed as we walked and talked about everything under the sun.

We took the bus to the large fairgrounds. It was jam-packed with people. Large tents were erected that would serve as beer tents. Beyond the several circus-style tents was the carnival. I could see carousels, Ferris wheels, and other rides. The first thing we did was buy a mug of beer. The scantily-dressed barmaids were each carrying 12 mugs of beer, six in each hand and happily delivering them to all the partygoers. Bitalo commented on the barmaids' strength and compared it to the villagers in Uganda carrying baskets on their heads.

Someone from the group said they were hungry, so we all headed inside one of the giant white tents. People were crammed to the rafters, making it difficult to maneuver around. We finally located a picnic table and quickly grabbed it. We listened to the band play traditional German music, watched the people drink beer, and we sang along with all the partygoers getting into the festive mood. Bitalo, Birdie, Grayson, and I were having the time of our lives.

Most of the German men were dressed in the traditional lederhosen and feathered hats and the women wore dirndl dresses. We stood out with our Levis and casual appearance, revealing that we were Americans. Bitalo made a comment that he didn't think he could pull off the lederhosen look. Everyone erupted in laughter.

We dined on sausages, pretzels, potato pancakes—and beer. After our stomachs had been filled, we ventured outside the tent to the carnival area. As we made our way to the carnival midway, we passed several game booths and more food booths.

"Look at the heart-shaped gingerbread cookies," I said to Grayson, breaking from holding hands and quickly making my way to the

cookie display. Soon the four of us were gazing at the colorfully decorated cookies.

Each cookie was equivalent to about six regular cookies, decorated
with icing and German sayings, and hung with ribbon and displayed. I
picked one that said "Ich liebe dich"—"I love you" in German. Grayson
and I nibbled on the cookie as we made our way deeper into the
carnival. I looked back and saw my friends holding hands, laughing,
and in between laughs taking bites of a gingerbread cookie of
their own.

The atmosphere at the carnival was loud and crazy. Music was
blaring under most of the tents, and the crowd noise was just as loud.
It was hard to hear yourself think let alone carry on a conversation.
However, in my ploy to continue to get to know Grayson, every
chance I had, I'd engage him in conversation to find out as much
about him as I could. Like most guys, he didn't talk a lot, and he didn't
say a lot about himself. It was up to me to get him to open up! I saw
Birdie and Bitalo make their way toward a carnival game and seeing
this as my chance, I cornered Grayson.

"Hey, you, come here." I gestured for him to come close. I wrapped
my arms around him. "Are you having a good time?" I asked as I
pulled him in and kissed his cheek.

"Yes, of course," he said kissing me lightly on the lips.

"It seems so surreal to be here in Germany and here at Oktoberfest. I'm glad we're here together," I added, kissing him back.

"I really like your friends. I'm glad they had an opportunity to
come out with us," he said, kissing me again. "Do you ever think about
one of us leaving?" he asked, gazing into my eyes.

"I try not to think about it. But yes, I realize it is probable."

"I don't know if I can bear to be without you, Jessica."

"Let's not think about that right now. It will ruin the festive mood
we're in." Feeling blue now that he'd brought up the possibility of one
of us leaving, I felt I needed to change the subject.

After several hours of food, drink, and fun, we headed back to the
bus stop that would take us home. The bus ride home was quiet. I
even heard some snoring. It was a fun night with many overindul-

gences. All of a sudden one of the revelers let out a combination snort and honk, waking several riders, causing one of the guys in our group to proclaim, "Damn, what was that?" We all erupted in laughter. I was sure there would be some hangovers in the morning.

One by one, we made our way down the aisle of the bus and out into the night air. We said our good nights and everyone went their separate ways. Crystal had dumped her date for the evening for Charles and they walked up ahead, laughing and cuddling just like old times. I guess they had one of those relationships that kept bringing them back to each other. Grayson grabbed my hand, and Bitalo, Birdie, and I made our way toward their hotel. We were chatting amongst ourselves, and in between, soft talking, soft kisses, and nibbles were taking place. I could see up ahead that Bitalo and Birdie were definitely in love. We finally reached their hotel.

"We had a great time, you two!" Bitalo remarked loudly.

Birdie nodded her head in agreement.

"How much longer will you be here in the country?" Grayson asked.

"Two more days," Birdie responded.

"Well, I'm sure we'll get together before you head back to Uganda."

We bid them good night, and I assured Birdie that we'd meet for dinner the following night. I told her we had some unfinished girl talk.

Grayson and I started the fifteen-minute walk to my house. Before reaching my home, Grayson suddenly stopped and pulled me close, and as our lips touched I detected a hint of gingerbread.

"Did you have a good time?" he asked, gazing into my eyes.

Muttering something that sounded like yes, I squeezed him tight, resting my head on his big strong shoulder. He released his hold, tilted my chin up, and gracefully planted another warm and moist kiss on my lips. He pulled me closer and soon his hands were gently gliding down my back and stopping just above my hips. We stood in that position for a few seconds, softly kissing one another, taking in every second of the experience and hoping it wouldn't end when finally he stopped, stepped back and looked into my eyes once again.

"Jessica … Jessica," he said as he stood there looking deep into my eyes.

I knew the frustration he felt. I was feeling it as well. Without saying any more, we continued walking the short distance to my house. I wanted to invite him up to my apartment, pull his clothes off, and make mad passionate love to him. I felt that strongly about him and about us. However, I didn't think it was fair to just ignore the fact that I had not been forthright with him and acknowledge that the memory of Josh had been keeping us apart. I couldn't in good conscience just fall into bed with him without an explanation. I owed him that much.

"Shh. Don't say anything," I said to him, taking his hands in mine. "I want to talk to you, but not tonight. I don't want the beer or the moment being the excuse for us doing something we may regret later, or not be ready for. I do want you to know that I care about you a great deal. I haven't been upfront with you about some things, and it's time to come clean. Can you come over tomorrow for brunch? I make a mean omelet," I said, trying to make light of a very serious moment. He gave me a light peck on the cheek and released my hands. I slowly turned up the walkway heading for the steps. When I got to the top of the steps, I turned around. "Ten thirty, and don't be late."

THE NEXT MORNING I was busily preparing our brunch when he arrived, right on time. I swung the door open and there he stood, holding the most beautiful bouquet of roses I'd ever seen. Motioning for him to enter, we made our way to the farm-style kitchen. I poured us each a cup of coffee and proceeded to whip up the omelets. Grayson's eyes grew big with amazement as I began flipping them from the frying pan to the plate.

"The biscuits and bacon are being kept warm in the oven. Could you get the oven mitt and get them out for me?"

Grayson did just as I'd asked and, even going a step further, found a towel, covered the biscuits, and set them on the table.

"This is the best ham and cheese omelet I think I've ever had," he exclaimed.

"My momma taught me how to make 'em."

"Your momma must be a great cook then."

I nodded my head; she was. We made small talk about the events of the previous night and how Charles and Crystal kept finding their way back to one another. I chalked it up to more of a need they both had and adding that I didn't think it was the healthiest way to have a relationship, but that it appeared to work for them. Grayson agreed. We finished our omelets and soon we were side by side doing the dishes.

"You wash and I'll dry and put away," he said, looking in a drawer for a clean towel.

I filled up the sink with hot soapy water and started scrubbing the plates. I turned toward him to hand him a dish covered in suds for rinsing when all of a sudden soapsuds splattered everywhere as he pulled me in for a kiss that I'd not soon forget. My heart was racing a mile a minute, our kiss leaving me breathless and wanting more. He gently separated my lips, teasing me with his tongue. I stroked his hair, and ran my hands up and down his back and arms—it was the most intense kiss we'd shared. After a few minutes of mindless kissing, we pulled apart at the same time. I reached up and put my hand to my mouth. It was soft and moist from his kisses.

"Grayson, there's something I need to tell you."

"Now? Can't it wait?" he asked, breathing hard.

"Yes, now!" I insisted, not really wanting to intrude on the moment, but knowing I needed to. "Sit down. I have to get something off my chest."

He begrudgingly sat down. He looked like a little boy whose ice cream melted before he could devour it.

"I just think it's important that you know where I'm coming from. I haven't been completely honest with you. I didn't want to share too much because I've been hurt in the past. I felt the less you knew about me, the better. I've really come to care about you, so now I want to open up to you."

He reached across the table and took my hands in his, gazing into my eyes for all the answers.

"I had a crush on a guy from back home. We joined the service together. I thought Josh was *the* one. He started acting strangely soon after we arrived in D.C. for training. I tried to move on from him and found myself in the arms of another man while in Africa."

Grayson listened intently.

"When I arrived here in Germany, I told myself no more guys. I just wanted to have fun. And who do I meet after only being here for a short time—you! I will admit to you now that I felt the chemistry between us, but I didn't want to let anything happen. When you all took me to Paris for my birthday, I was happy you thought that much of me, but I was also sad. See, Paris is where Josh and I had talked about going as a couple. I was bummed that it wasn't the two of us traipsing through the streets of Paris, or that it wasn't the two of us sharing a hotel room."

Grayson let go of my hands.

"Don't misunderstand me, Grayson. I had a great time in Paris with you. I just wished I could've let go of all the baggage I was carrying around regarding Josh and Andrew."

"Andrew?"

"Andrew—the guy I knew in Africa."

Grayson nodded that he understood. "What do you want to do? Where do you want this relationship to go?" he asked with a tone of concern in his voice.

"That's just it. I want to be with you," I said with an urgency that surprised even me. "I contacted Josh last week. I'd been putting it off, but realized he was what was standing in the way of our happiness. I found him on the State Department's locator database. He's living in France. He's happily married, and soon to be a father. I have the closure I needed and now I can commit to our relationship ..." I said, trailing off and realizing I was just rambling now.

He reached for my hands once again. He carefully stroked my thumb with his fingers and I felt a tingling sensation all the way down to my toes. I wanted him badly.

"No more cold shoulder. No more *let's take it slow*," he voiced.

This time, I started stroking his hand, and soon I was making my way up his arm, circling the hairs on his forearm with my fingers. He stood up, pushing the chair back with his legs and pulling me up at the same time. We embraced for a moment and he kissed me, giving me chills that ran up and down my spine. We were the only ones in my apartment so we could've had our way with each other on the kitchen table and no one would've known. We both knew it was a bit too soon for that. We definitely made progress and that left both of us wanting more, but willing to wait … for the right moment. It would happen. We both knew it. It had to be perfect, though.

The next evening, as planned, we met Bitalo and Birdie for dinner. We laughed and talked about old times. Soon it was time for them to head back to their hotel. I took this opportunity to tell her more about Grayson.

"Listen, Birdie. I don't know exactly where this is headed with Grayson, but I can tell you it's hot and steamy and we're about to take our relationship to the next level," I said breathlessly.

She looked at me with her eyes bulging, like she couldn't believe what I was saying.

"You, *Miss I can't commit*, are telling me that you're about to seriously commit?" she marveled, searching me hard for confirmation she heard me right.

I nodded my head. "I feel something for him that I'd not felt before. I think I love him," I spit out.

"I'm happy for you, Jessica. Please keep in touch, and let me know how things are going. Let's not be strangers. We've come too far to let distance get in the way of our friendship."

I nodded and hugged her with all my might. I gently pushed her back. "See? That's what I love about you. You're such a true friend. I felt it from the first time I saw you sitting on the bed in D.C." I said, smiling as I recalled that day.

CHAPTER 16

*W*e were like two lovesick birds. We probably made people gag with our behavior. Thankfully, no one said anything or I might have popped them one. I was madly in love with this boy and nothing or nobody would get in my way. We were inseparable. Any day that Grayson was in town, he'd wait for me at the bench and walk me home. When he had to go in the field and play war games, I missed him. They say absence makes the heart grow fonder— and it did. We made up for all the lost time together.

He was gentle and experienced and I was naïve and not. We made a great couple. Our desire for one another was hot and steamy despite my lack of experience. I caught on fast, and it felt natural to be with him. Once he started kissing me, I'd melt into his big strong arms. We'd end up showing each other how much we loved each other and then, spent from all the activity, fall asleep in each other's arms.

Just like on most days, Grayson was waiting for me at the bench. But this time, he was standing and I could see from a distance he was pacing. As I got closer, I saw a look of concern on his face telling me something was wrong. I picked up my pace to get to him quicker. Little did I know, I'd be the one who'd need comforting.

"Why the long face—is everything okay?" I asked, knowing that it wasn't.

"I got orders. I'm leaving Germany."

It took me a few seconds to process his words. "Leaving Germany … leaving me…" I trailed off. "Where is the Army sending you?" I asked, trying to be strong.

"California. Monterey, California."

"California! You're going back home?"

"Well, it's not really that close to home. I'll be about five hours from home," he corrected, letting me know that wasn't the real issue.

"Grayson, I can't bear to think about you going. I need you," I said, sounding a bit desperate.

"Jessica, come with me to California. Let's get married," he whispered in my ear as he pulled me close.

I can admit now those were the exact words I wanted to hear, but after I heard them, I couldn't imagine them really materializing. There were too many obstacles in our way to make his suggestion become a reality.

"I can't come to California with you, Grayson. I have a job here in Frankfurt. I can't just quit. I love my job here, and well …" I said, trailing off because I didn't know what else to say.

"I thought you loved me," he said, looking deeply into my eyes with a look of sadness.

"I do love you. It's just awful timing." I added, hoping that would make our situation less awkward and yet show him I cared.

We walked to my apartment in silence, holding hands. I kept hearing his words playing over and over in my mind, telling me he was leaving. I don't know why we were so shocked. It was bound to happen. His being in the Army and the possibility of relocating was always on my mind and the main reason I wasn't sure I wanted to develop a relationship with him.

We entered the apartment. I put my coat in the closet, moved to the kitchen, and began to boil water for tea. Grayson sat down at the table in the kitchen. It felt as if someone had died. I fixed two mugs of hot tea and set one in front of him. I took a seat across from him.

"Grayson, talk to me."

"I'm at a loss for words right now. I guess I thought you'd say yes. I'm not sure where to go from here," he said sadly, stirring his tea with his finger.

"I just can't leave right now." I got up from my seat and went over to him. I kneeled down and got his attention. "I love you with all my heart. I really do."

I gave him several gentle pecks on the cheek, ending up with my lips pressed against his. He moved his body slightly in the chair to better position himself to kiss me back. Our kiss became passionate; he pulled me up, and soon we were in the bedroom. He pulled his shirt out of his uniform pants and quickly unbuckled his belt. Still connected by our lips, we continued to undress each other with such frenzy—our clothes and shoes ending up in every corner of the room. We finally fell onto the bed and soon we were under the covers in a tangled mess.

We held each other tight, trying to make sense out of what had occurred—was it out of love, or was it out of desperation? We both knew this might be the end of us. We knew relationships didn't hold up well with thousands of miles separating couples. I was willing to try, though. I owed him that much. He owed me that much as well.

The next few weeks were busy for him. He had to wrap up all the loose ends regarding his job and get his household items packed and ready for pick up. He shared with me the information he received about Monterey. It seemed like a lovely place to live.

In all of our discussions about the new assignment, he'd always add, "when you come for a visit." I nodded. "Yes, when I come for a visit," I echoed.

I recall the day he left as if it was yesterday. It was a sad day for both of us. I remember that, in anticipation of him leaving, I got myself all worked up and made myself ill. I couldn't believe this was happening to us. After a romantic dinner at a local gasthaus, we went back to my apartment and loved the night away. The next morning I offered to fix him breakfast, but neither one of us was hungry. We walked to the bus stop. The anticipation of him leaving was overwhelming. I held him for a long time; no words were spoken, just our bodies connected, feeling the sadness of the moment. The bus arrived shortly after we did. The doors opened, letting people off first. We stood back and let the others that were waiting board first. I wanted every second with him that I could have. The bus driver got out of his seat and came to the door.

"You better get on now if you want a ride to the airport."

"This is it, Jessica—time for me to head out."

I felt a huge lump forming in my throat, making it difficult to speak. I nodded that I understood it was time for him to leave.

"Write me. Call me. Visit me," he said pushing out short quick demands to ensure I heard them all before the door to the bus closed. "I love you, Jessica," he called out to me as he stepped backward onto the bus's steps.

I mouthed the words back. My throat felt like it had been ripped wide open and was raw for the entire world to see. Tears rolled down my cheeks. I waved to Grayson as he walked down the aisle of the bus to take his seat.

The bus started to pull away, but not before I got one last glimpse of Grayson. I ran a short distance alongside the bus, waving to him, and shouting out, "I love you!"

Finally, when I couldn't see the bus any longer, I sat down on the bench at the bus stop and wept. I couldn't believe this was happening to me again. I was so close to a commitment that I could taste it. In one instant, the commitment was ripped from my heart and I wasn't sure if I'd ever be the same again. I sat on the bench for a long time. Watching him leave on the bus with his duffle bag was so surreal. I finally gathered all my thoughts, put them in the back corner of my mind, and made the trek home. I was in a daze as I walked, trying to figure out what my next plan of action would be.

I entered my apartment and, although Grayson had never lived with me, it felt cold and lonely, as if he had moved out. I sat on the sofa, collecting my thoughts and wondering where the bus was or if he was at the airport yet. I visualized him waiting in line, going through customs, and having his passport stamped. All the things I went through when I traveled. I let out a loud sigh that even startled me. I ventured into the kitchen and fixed myself a cup of tea.

The tea helped some, but my mood was far from cheery. My boyfriend had just left and I was heartbroken. I decided to turn in early for the night. Feeling somewhat depressed, sleep seemed the best option. I showered and got ready for bed, skipping dinner, and fell fast asleep after reading a couple of chapters of my latest romance novella.

THE NEXT SEVERAL WEEKS, I went through the motions of being present both at work and in my social circles. It was hard, though. I waited in breathless anticipation for a letter from Grayson. I knew the mail was slow coming from the States, but that didn't seem to comfort me. Finally, a letter came.

DEAR JESSICA,

I'VE ARRIVED at my duty station, Monterey, California. The weather is rainy and cool. The base is spread out, and so far, I've met some nice people. I miss you so much!

Please write back soon.

LOVE,
Grayson

I KEPT RE-READING the few sentences over and over. I was hoping he'd write more. I knew his career kept him extremely busy, but I was hoping for a few more words from him. I immediately sat down and drafted a letter to him.

. . .

Dear Grayson,

I'm so happy to have received your letter. I've been a mess since you've left. I can't sleep, I hardly eat, and I'm not good company for anyone! I can't wait to see you and have you hold me in your arms. Please write again soon. Send me pictures of Monterey, too.

Love you always,
Jessica

CRYSTAL TRIED to cheer me up by inviting me to go out to a local pub with her and a few of our co-workers. At first, I said no, but then I decided that drowning my sorrows in a cold beer sounded pretty good. Everyone was lively and laughing and having a great time. Beer and music were always a good combination, it seemed. I tried to get in on the action, but it was of no use. I was a downer, for sure. I finished my beer and excused myself from the group.

"Thanks for inviting me, guys," I said as I gathered my things to head out the door. "I'm just not in that festive a mood."

Crystal jumped up, came over, and gave me a hug.

"Aww, Jessica. It'll get better soon. It's always hard when they first leave."

I gently pushed her away. "I doubt it."

Days turned into weeks, and weeks turned into months. I received, on average, a letter a week from Grayson. I waited eagerly for those letters. It was what kept me going. Each letter got longer and longer, and he even included some pictures. Our letters started out innocent enough, but like any couple that had been intimate, our conversations soon included statements like what I'd like to do to you, etc. It got me stirred up, that's for sure, so I can only imagine what it did to him!

I had a few guys try to fill in for Grayson, but I quickly let them know I wasn't interested. I mean, really? Did they think I was going to fall for some other guy just because my man wasn't physically here? If anything, my love grew even stronger with his absence. I thought about him day and night.

I was sitting at my desk when the phone rang. It was Grayson! I was so happy to hear his voice. We made small talk, he gave me his number at work, and then he said the words I had been waiting for. He asked me to come to California for a visit. I promised him I'd put in for the leave with my supervisor and notify him with the itinerary after I'd purchased my ticket.

"I love you, Jessica."

"I love you more."

My supervisor approved my leave for two weeks. I went over to the travel office and purchased my ticket to California.

Crystal knew something had changed. I was now smiling, interacting more, and lovely to be around, as she nicely put it. The next couple of weeks were torture for Grayson and me. We called each other almost every day now that we'd figured out the phone system. Just hearing his voice put me at ease, but at the same time made my heart beat faster. I don't quite remember the bus ride to the airport. I don't even remember waiting in the long line as customs checked my passport and allowed me access to the gate. I don't remember much of anything, as I was focused on Grayson. I couldn't wait to see him. I'd never felt like this with anyone before. I knew it was true love. With Josh, it was more of a high school crush, and with Andrew, it was more about loving and admiring what he did as a missionary. With Grayson, it was about loving the man.

CHAPTER 17

$\mathcal{G}$rayson picked me up at the San Francisco airport. It was foggy, drizzly, and cold, but even the weather couldn't dampen my spirits! I could see Grayson waiting for me amongst the many families and friends waiting for their loved ones. I started waving frantically at him, my smile growing larger with every step closer to him. Finally, I reached him and hugged him, taking in the sweet smell of his freshly starched uniform and aftershave. He gently pushed me away, planting a gentle, warm kiss on my lips.

"You look fantastic, Jessica."

"I'm so happy to see you," I said, squeezing him gently.

The ride to Monterey was surreal. I was with my baby now, and all I could think about was how happy he made me. He showed me some sights along the way, but they didn't really register. I hoped he'd show them to me again—I knew they were worth seeing.

"I rented a room for us—right on the beach."

"That sounds lovely," I said, taking his hand and rubbing it gently.

"I wish the weather would cooperate better. We have a lot of foggy days here, though," he added.

"It can pour down rain, I don't care. As long as I'm in your arms, the weather is fabulous!" I said, sounding like one lovestruck girl. He smiled that beautiful warm smile of his. I felt my stomach tighten, my blood start to heat, and my face felt red-hot.

He pulled up to the quaint hotel and parked the car. He retrieved my one piece of luggage from the trunk and led me straight to our room. He'd already picked up the key. He opened the door and I walked in. Sitting on the desk was a gorgeous vase full of colorful flowers.

"Oh! How beautiful, Grayson!"

"I thought you'd like them," he said, beaming.

I hardly got my jacket off before our lips locked in one intense, head-spinning make out session. Soon we were tugging on each other's clothes, shoes were being kicked off into a corner, and shirts practically ripped off, until finally we were a huddled mass under the covers. I knew I was a willing participant, but it was so wild and crazy that I'm short on details, but just remembered it was too good and too hot to control. Laying in his arms afterward, listening to him softly breathing, I felt like the luckiest woman in the entire universe.

We later went out for dinner at a lovely seaside restaurant. We dined on the local catch and drank a glass of California wine, a wonderful cabernet sauvignon. I had a ravenous appetite brought on by our voracious lovemaking—and also from the mere fact that I'd not been eating much since Grayson had left Germany.

We toasted to being reunited. "Here's to our love, may it never diminish."

Blushing, because gazing into his eyes reminded me of our passionate session, I tenderly spoke. "Cheers, Grayson. I love you."

Most of the two weeks were spent under the covers. The weather was a bit dreary for sightseeing, but we did our best. We took long walks on the beach in between rain showers, and I collected some beautiful shells. We stayed in bed until lunchtime, cuddled up, and reminiscing about our childhoods, where I learned much more about Grayson and he about me. I even told him about my uncle.

"Don't let that creep get anywhere near you, Jessica. I don't know what I'll do to him," he said heatedly.

"Don't worry. I won't let him," I replied matter-of-factly.

We talked about our dreams, our goals, and we discovered that we had so many similarities it was crazy. I was sad when the day came that I had to board the plane for Germany.

"I don't want to go, Grayson," I said, pouting.

"I know, babe. I don't want you to go either," he said, hugging me close, and making me feel secure in his strong arms.

"You have some decisions to make. I hope you'll decide for us," he said, gazing deep into my eyes, hoping for an answer right on the spot.

I nodded. My throat felt dry, and I could feel the tears forming in my eyes.

THE PHONE CALLS CAME DAILY. It was the same conversation for both of us. We missed each other, and couldn't wait to be together again. He never put any pressure on me to quit my job, but secretly I wished he would. However, I realized he'd never expect me to do something I didn't want to do. He admired me for the independent, strong woman that I was. Fortunately for us, Grayson wouldn't have to pressure me. The service did it for him.

CHAPTER 18

a short time after I got back from California, I received an assignment to Korea. Korea! As fascinating a place as that might be, it wouldn't be fascinating enough to keep me from Grayson. I contacted him and told him the news.

"What are you going to do?" he asked.

"I think I'm going to give my notice and resign," I said, testing his reaction.

"That would be awesome, Jessica, but only if that is what you really want—I know you could get another job here, probably on the base, too," he added eagerly.

THE NEXT COUPLE of weeks were a whirlwind. I gave the State Department notice that I'd be resigning from my job. They were sorry to see me go but were more concerned about the big holiday open house I was coordinating for the Amerika Haus. I assured them that all the plans were set in motion and that they'd have no trouble seeing them through. The dignitaries had been invited, reservations made, and menus decided. They just had to show up.

I spent my last few days packing up my apartment, and spending a little time with Crystal. She was happy for us but said she'd miss me. I wasn't convinced she'd miss me as much as she'd miss the fun times we had. She always had to be busy doing something, and she wasn't as concerned with who she was doing it with as much as she was concerned with what it was she'd be doing.

I was soon on my way to California, but this time, I'd be staying. I was excited about what the future held for us, and the possibility of us getting married.

On the ride back from the airport, Grayson told me he'd rented a small apartment. My eyes lit up.

"Our own apartment?" I asked.

"It's pretty bare right now, but I thought you could put your touch on it."

"I'd love to decorate it. I'll find just the right things to make it homey."

He drove up to a small apartment complex consisting of about ten units, a couple of blocks from the marina. We parked the car in our one designated parking spot—he was so proud of this and had to point it out to me as he retrieved my luggage from the trunk. I immediately took a deep whiff of the fresh air, realizing I'd missed it in the short time I'd been gone. We walked hand in hand up the stairs that would lead us to our second-floor apartment.

"This is perfect," I said as I ran from the living room to the kitchen, to the bedroom and back into the small dining area. "I can't wait to go shopping."

Our first night in our little apartment was special. I was so happy to be in the arms of my man. Exhausted from my long flight, I must have dozed off while he was talking to me. The next thing I remember was the aroma of coffee in the morning.

While Grayson was at work, I'd scout out the town and see what I could find to help furnish and decorate our humble abode. However, the first order of business was to call Momma and let her know I was back in the States, and that I had moved in with Grayson. I wasn't sure how she'd take the moving in part, but I was a grown woman making my own decisions. I felt even if she didn't approve, she'd respect my decision. Just as I had suspected, she was happy that I was in the States but cautious about showing her approval of us living together. I let her know that Grayson and I were talking about getting married, and that seemed to smooth things over. After we hung up the phone, I felt relieved that I was able to tell her all about the love of my life and my upcoming marriage.

Over the next couple of weeks, I was busy decorating to the best of our meager budget's ability. I found some charming things at a secondhand store in town, and the rest of it we picked up at the local discount store. I tried to keep busy while Grayson was out at the base. It only took me about twenty minutes to clean the apartment, leaving me with a lot of free time. I'd eventually find a job, but having just moved to a new place, I decided to wait for a bit.

I was getting used to the unusual weather in Monterey. Most of the time clouds hung overhead and a thick fog blanketed the town, mixed in with a light drizzle. I had been forewarned that the weather in the wintertime was wet, but thankfully it wasn't snowing! We only had one car, so I learned the bus system to take me to most places. Or I would walk down to the marina, as it was close by. It wasn't a very large area and I enjoyed watching the seagulls flapping their wings and diving into the water looking for their next meal. It was completely different from any of the places I'd lived before.

In the evening, we'd cuddle on the couch, watch movies, and look at bridal and wedding books that I'd checked out from the local library. We'd pretty much decided on our wedding date—the fifth of June. We had six months to purchase the dress, reserve a place for the reception, and send out our invitations.

"Who do you want to invite?" I asked as I wrote down Momma, then Lauren, Birdie, Bitalo, and Crystal with a question mark beside their names.

"I guess my parents and siblings ..." he said, fidgeting on the couch. "In fact, I thought we should go see them."

"Okay. I'd like to meet your folks."

130

"I just want to warn you. They're a bit odd," he said, chuckling.
"They can't be any odder than my momma and crazy uncle."

CHAPTER 19

$\mathcal{I}$ found Grayson's parents to be delightful. I sensed the strain in their relationship, though. I tried to smooth the way, and I think I did a good job. His mom told me stories of his childhood and even brought out the dreaded photo album.

"Geez, Mom, do you have to pull out the pictures, too?" Grayson said with some fun-loving irritation in his voice.

"You were an adorable child," his mom said proudly, pointing to the photo of Grayson dressed up as a cowboy.

After looking at pictures and making small talk, they suggested taking us out to dinner. It was okay with me. I liked to eat out. The weather was a lot different in Los Angeles. It was warm, and the sun came out just about every day we were there. I guess it was true as the song, "It never rains in Southern California."

Grayson took me to the beach and showed me where he used to surf. It was beautiful. I took my shoes off and walked through the sand, letting it press up in between my toes. I found some beautiful shells that the morning's tide had brought in. Later, the locals lined up on the beach, decked out in their bathing suits and gleaming boards ready to hit the waves, which gave me a glimpse of what Grayson had looked like during his surfing days. I tried to study his body language to see if there were any signs he was happy or sad to be back here.

"Do you miss surfing?"

"I do," he said, gazing out at the water, watching the big waves roll in.

"You shouldn't give up something you love," I said, lacing my arm into his. "I could never give up reading my books."

"I know. If I really wanted to get back into it, I could. I think I might try something different. Life is about experiences, and surfing was just one of the many I have on my resume," he said. He cupped his hand over mine and gently squeezed it.

"I just don't want you to have any regrets," I whispered.

"No regrets, Jessica. I can promise you that," he said, dropping a quick kiss on my forehead.

We headed back to the Grayson's parents' house. It was alive with chatter from lots of family who'd dropped in. Soon we were sitting around the table and I was hearing once again the stories of Grayson's youth.

We left Grayson's family after a few days but vowed to return when we could stay longer. His mom offered to help with the wedding plans and I told her I'd be in touch. There really wasn't much to do. We'd planned a very simple wedding.

"Your folks were nice, Grayson. Thanks for taking me to meet them." I smiled and reached out and patted him on the leg as he was driving. He took one of his hands off the steering wheel and gently touched my hand.

"Hey! Keep both hands on the wheel, mister!" I said, chuckling.

It was 1980, and besides my wedding, it was another eventful year—Ronald Reagan was elected as President, and a deranged fan assassinated John Lennon. New sounds came out from Blondie, Devo, and something new—rap by a group called Sugar Hill Gang, and the weekly television show *Dallas* had millions of viewers tuning in to find out "Who shot J.R.?" Looking back, I liked the eighties.

Planning a wedding on a budget was hard work. I had lots of free time on my hands so doing the research on how to make our money stretch became a challenge.

Out of the blue, we received a check from Grayson's parents for five thousand dollars to help with the costs.

"This is outrageous!" I said to Grayson as he shared the news.

"I told you. My parents are over the top with stuff," he said, slightly disgusted.

"I feel bad taking this money. My momma can't even begin to compete with this, Grayson."

"No need to feel bad, Jessica. If they want to toss the money our way, we'll use it. We didn't ask for a cent of their money. Let's just use it for the wedding like they asked."

"Well … I've pretty much budgeted for most of the wedding, but maybe we can invite a few more guests, and have a nice honeymoon?"

"That sounds like a great idea!"

During the day, I scouted out certain venues that would be appropriate for our reception. To save money, we decided to ask the base chaplain to officiate. We decided on two large vases that would sit on the floor filled with colorful flowers, and I purchased satin ribbon to make bows for the pews.

Our guest list was small, so finding a place for the reception would be easy. I was looking for restaurants that had large banquet areas that could accommodate fifty people. Grayson's family and friends would fill most of the seats. He had cousins, aunts and uncles, and of course, his parents, grandparents, and siblings. My momma and Lauren would come for me. I knew neither Crystal nor Birdie would be able to attend, but I'd send them an invitation just the same. Some of Grayson's buddies from Germany rotated to Monterey with him, so he asked if they could come.

"Of course, you can invite your friends. This is your wedding, too!" I teased.

"I guess I'll invite a couple of my friends from my surfing days, too."

I could see that the guest list would be mainly his friends and family, but that was okay with me. I just wanted to be his wife.

I was sitting at the table going over things when the doorbell rang. The mail carrier was standing on my porch with a large box.

"Please sign here," he directed.

I walked back into the apartment, trying to read where the box came from. I immediately recognized the return address. It was from Momma. I tore open the box, anxious to see what was in it. I pulled back the white tissue paper and a garment of some type, folded neatly lay in the box. I lifted the garment out and realized it was a wedding dress. Classic in design, the dress was tea-length and I could tell that it was not new. In the bottom of the box, in Momma's handwriting, I found an envelope. I opened it.

DEAR JESSICA,

THIS WAS *my wedding dress many years ago. I wasn't sure if you wanted to wear it or not. It will need cleaning and unfortunately, I can't afford to do that. There are some loose threads, and some repair work necessary, but if you think it's worth fixing, you may have the dress.*

Love, Momma

I CLUTCHED the letter to my chest and looked over at the slightly yellowed dress. Thoughts came flooding in of Momma and Daddy getting married, and I could picture Momma wearing the dress and saying "I do." I bet she was the happiest person in the world at that moment. I still wasn't sure why he'd left us, and I probably would never know. It was a hard thing to live with knowing your daddy walked out on you.

CHAPTER 20

Time flew by and soon I realized we were thirty days out from the big day. I had organized everything and felt confident it would turn out nicely. It was going to be a small wedding. I only had one bridesmaid, Lauren, and Grayson chose one of his brothers to be his best man. Just as we'd thought, we had about fifty guests RSVP. The reception would be at a lovely restaurant on the boulevard facing the bay. Grayson and I took some of the money his parents gave us and purchased Momma's plane ticket. He said it would be our little secret. His generosity made me swell with happiness. He was so special, and Momma was going to love him.

We also decided to take some of the money and upgrade our honeymoon. We initially were just going to stay in a hotel in downtown Monterey, overlooking the bay, but after his parents had sent us the money, I started looking around. I'd always wanted to go to Bodega Bay, as I'd read about it in many books. Grayson agreed it would be a wonderful place for a honeymoon.

Momma and Lauren arrived a few days early to help me with any last-minute details. Grayson was such a gentleman and, just as I'd predicted, Momma and Lauren loved him. I'd made reservations at a budget hotel for them, as our apartment was just too small. They seemed pleased with the accommodations. They quickly freshened up, an, eager to help, expressed that they were ready to tie some bows. We headed to our apartment where we spent a couple of hours laughing and making bows. Lauren and Momma couldn't get over the weather.

"It's foggy in the morning, but by the afternoon, it's gorgeous!" Lauren exclaimed.

Momma agreed.

We headed out to the church so they could see the modest setup. I showed them where the flowers would go, and I showed them how I wanted the bows placed at the end of each pew.

"Are we picking up the flowers?" Momma asked.

"No, they'll be delivered the morning of. We went with large white urn-shaped vases, and I selected purple, white, and shades of pink flowers with a touch of greenery. Bright and colorful," I added.

Both Momma and Lauren nodded their heads as they visualized the beauty of the flowers.

Our next stop was the restaurant. I just wanted them to see the general layout.

"This outdoor space is great! It's so ... California," Lauren squealed.

"Over here we'll have a long buffet table set up. Here, there will be seven large round tables with white linen and a small table decoration —I went with a hurricane-style candle decoration with a little greenery," I added. "Over there," I gestured, "will be the DJ."

"Sounds lovely, Jessica," Momma said, sounding a little emotional.

Sensing she needed a hug, I embraced her.

"Let's head back to the apartment. I have something I want to show you."

Grayson was over at the large house his parents had rented for their stay. It had eight bedrooms so that all the family could stay under one roof. I was blown away by the magnitude of the house and wondered how someone could be so wealthy to own something so magnificent.

I called Momma and Lauren into our bedroom. I opened the closet door to retrieve the dry-cleaning bag and started to unzip it. I could hear Momma gasp. She knew what it was before I even took it out. I gently held it up against my body so they could get the idea of what it would look like on me.

Momma couldn't believe how beautiful her dress looked.

"The yellow is gone. It looks brand-new," she said, running her fingers up and down the dress.

"I found a dressmaker who repaired the dress, and she recommended a dry cleaner that specialized in wedding dresses. I just love it, and can't wait for you to see me in it."

I looked up to see a couple of tears rolling down Momma's face. I wasn't completely sure, but I bet she was thinking about Daddy. I hugged her and gently pushed her back to look softly into her eyes.

"I hope those are tears of happiness, Momma." I figured deep down inside they weren't, but I needed to get the mood happy again. "I'm so thankful to you, Momma. You raised me good! You allowed me to grow, and for that, I'll always be grateful. You wanted me to have what you didn't, and that is the sign of a great parent."

"I'm glad you feel that way. It wasn't always easy, that's for sure. I tried my best to give you a good homelife. I know Uncle wasn't the best to you, and I'm sorry that I didn't realize it sooner. You think you know someone, and you really don't," she added sadly. "I didn't want to tell you, but I think you're strong enough to handle this. Uncle is ill —his drinking is doing him in. He'll have to answer to the good Lord for his sins."

We never spoke of Uncle again after that day. Momma *did* know. She wasn't ignoring my uneasiness about him. She was silently taking care of the issue. It made me happy to know she believed me, but I was sad she'd soon lose her sole sibling.

The next two days were spent visiting and showing them around Monterey. With everything done, we were just waiting for the day. Grayson spent the night with his family in their enormous mansion and Momma and Lauren stayed with me. The three of us in that small apartment was interesting. Momma and I shared the bed, and Lauren slept on our gently-used sofa.

We stayed up until the wee hours of the morning reminiscing

about our childhood and it didn't really sound so boring now. It reminded me of an old adage, *The grass isn't always greener on the other side!*

The following morning, Lauren and I were dragging. We made the coffee and while sipping the hot beverage at the table, Lauren reached across and took my hands in hers.

"I'm so happy for you, Jessica. I know we've not done a very good job of keeping in touch, but that doesn't really matter now. We're together again."

"I know. I haven't done my best in that regard. I guess I was running away from what I thought was an awful life, but actually just finding out it was quite normal—except for my uncle. Momma told me he's dying."

"Jessica, all of us have had to find our way—discover who we are and why things occurred the way they did. I'm thankful I went away to college. I met wonderful people and I also got to see how others lived—and you're right, many of them not so differently than you and me. Some people would think your life has been exciting, traveling abroad and seeing and experiencing all that you have."

"I wouldn't trade a thing, Lauren. I wouldn't have met Grayson if I'd stayed in Texas."

"True. I'm so glad you met him. I just love him to pieces!" she squealed.

"Yes, Lauren, we've been through how much you love him," I teased, shaking my head.

Momma came out of the bathroom, towel drying her hair.

"Come on, you two! You're going to be late for your own wedding!" Momma shouted to us.

Lauren and I looked at Momma and then looked at the clock. We'd been chatting for almost an half hour. We both pushed our chairs out from the table.

"You go first, Lauren."

Just then there was a light rap on the front door. I had suspected it was Grayson. I opened the door and couldn't believe my eyes. Standing before me were Birdie and Bitalo! They'd made it!

"Oh, my God! It's really you! You made it!" I exclaimed as I pulled them both into the apartment.

Momma and Lauren looked at each other, trying to figure out what was going on.

"Momma, this is Birdie, my dear friend I met in D.C. and who later went to Africa with me."

We quickly made the introductions and then I told them I had to help Momma get ready.

I helped Momma get dressed. She'd selected a casual dress; we Texans are practical people. It was a vast improvement over the checkered housedress and apron she usually wore. Lauren chose a casual sleeveless shift that she looked beautiful in with her long, lean legs.

We arrived at the church with not much time to spare. Lauren helped me get into Momma's dress.

"You look beautiful, Owl," she said, laughing.

"I haven't heard that name in years," I said.

"You're going to be the happiest couple. I just love Grayson," she said in her thick Texas drawl.

We waited behind the curtain for the music to queue my entrance. I heard the organist start to play the wedding march. It was bittersweet. I knew most brides had their dads walk them down the aisle. I had my momma. It didn't matter that much to me; it had been Momma and me for a long time.

We made our way down the aisle, slowly walking to the song. As I walked past the pews, I saw the familiar faces of new acquaintances and old friends, Birdie and Bitalo, and of course, Lauren. I could see Grayson standing at the front waiting for me, his best man standing next to him. Lauren looked so radiant in her attire, waiting for us to arrive. The walk seemed long to me as my mind wandered over the last several years.

Momma handed my arm to Grayson. We stood side by side and as the chaplain spoke the words that would unite us as husband and wife, I thought about how fortunate I really was. My family, as small as it was, meant the world to me, and I was grateful for Momma and everything she'd done for me. It's not easy being a single parent. Money was always tight, but we made the best of it.

We exchanged rings—simple gold bands—and when the chaplain said, "You may kiss the bride," I remember looking into Grayson's gorgeous eyes and feeling his soft lips sealing the deal. I was one happy gal!

Our reception was like a big barbecue with friends. Everyone was eating, drinking, and thumping their feet to the music the DJ played. Over and over we heard how beautiful the wedding and the reception were. Grayson and I couldn't stop beaming. We'd done it. We'd made it. I found myself squeezing him every now and then during the night to make sure I wasn't dreaming.

Grayson and I were not heading out to Bodega Bay until the following day. We had to get Momma and Lauren to the airport for their trip home first. We dropped them off at their hotel, promising to see them in the morning. "We can stop and have breakfast somewhere, okay?" I asked as we dropped them off.

"Sounds good, kids," Momma said.

It wasn't like we were strangers in the bedroom, but tonight was going to be special because now we were husband and wife. I was anticipating that it would be different, but what I didn't predict was how emotional I'd be afterward.

Grayson held me as I cried softly in his arms, reassuring me that he'd love me forever—and forever was a very long time! I knew our life was going to be great, and I couldn't wait to get started as his wife —his life partner.

"I love you, Grayson. I'm so glad you persevered to win me over. I was such a wreck back then."

"I didn't know initially how much you'd mean to me, but it wasn't long before I knew."

I moved forward, our lips touching in another soft moment.

We arrived in Bodega Bay in the early evening. It was a beautiful summer evening as we observed the silver-gray fogbank contrasting dramatically with the setting sun.

I'd made the reservation through a vacation-by-owner service. The owner, Libby, said we could check in at a little café and pick up the key. We found the Seaside Café and walked in. The wind chime on the door jingled, letting the employees know someone had entered. We waited about a minute before a young woman came out to greet us.

"Two for dinner?"

"Actually … I'm looking for Avery. We're here to pick up a key for the house that Libby owns."

"Oh, you're the honeymooners! Yes, I have the key. Just a moment." She came back with a key and handed it to us.

"Thank you," I said.

"Listen, Libby wanted me to invite you to have dinner here tonight, on the house—that's if you've not eaten yet."

Grayson and I looked at each other. We hadn't had time to think about dinner.

"That is very nice of her … of you. Thank you," I said.

"Follow me. I have just the perfect table for you."

We followed Avery to a booth near the window. The moonlight was bouncing off the water and providing just enough light to see the boats harbored for the night. She gave us menus and filled our glasses with water.

"You can have anything you like, but I have to suggest the clam chowder to start. People come from miles around for a bowl of this steamy, delicious soup."

Grayson and I took Avery up on her suggestion. That night, we learned all about Libby and the *Salty Dog*.

It was very dark by the time we arrived at Libby's place. A beam of light from the full moon allowed us to see some of the outside. It wouldn't be until the morning that we'd get the full picture of how charming it truly was. Once we entered the cottage we both instantly felt a sense of familiarity as if we'd been there before. We both headed toward the French doors where we could see a glimpse of that full moon. I threw open the doors and we both stepped out on to the deck. I took in a deep breath of the ocean air and let it out slowly. Grayson pulled me close as we admired the moon and the bay that was just barely visible by moonlight.

"I'm so glad you thought of Bodega Bay," he said, hugging me tighter.

I nodded. "Me, too."

"I really like the little café, and that chowder ... it was delicious," Grayson remarked.

"I'd love the recipe."

I shivered slightly, the cool night air beginning to chill the night.

"Let's go inside and warm up," Grayson said.

We made our way back into the main living area. We both saw it at the same time. Sitting on the glass and wood coffee table sat a big beautiful basket with a large purple bow, filled with fruit, cheese, and wine. A soft yellow envelope with our names sat beside the basket. I reached for it, taking out the handwritten note that was inside.

DEAR HONEYMOONERS GRAYSON AND JESSICA!

WE HOPE you enjoy your stay at the Seaside Cottage. If you need anything don't hesitate to let Avery know. Don't forget to sign the guest book.

LIBBY

"HOW THOUGHTFUL," I said as I peered deep inside the basket.

Grayson was soon rummaging for something in one of the kitchen drawers.

"What are you looking for?" I asked.

He looked up at me from across the open wall that divided the kitchen from the living space. A warm and sensual smile moved across his face. Soon, the familiar sound of a cork popping out of a bottle followed by gurgling sounds of wine being poured filled the rooms of the quiet cottage.

We sat next to each other on the sofa, and after a toast, I made the announcement of how happy I was.

"It wasn't so much that I was unhappy in West Texas, as I felt sheltered and isolated. I knew by reading all those books that there was something more, out beyond my little town."

Grayson nodded. He pulled me closer to him. "I know, babe. You were just searching for new happiness, is all."

I nodded. I turned toward him slightly so I could focus on his eyes. "It's true."

He tilted his head and narrowed his eyes. "True? True about what?"

"Happiness is where you hang your hat." I laughed at my silly statement.

Grayson held up his wine glass. I gently tapped the rim of his glass with my own. "To Happiness," he said.

"To Happiness," I repeated, and then I leaned in for a kiss.

We didn't realize it at the time, but we'd become frequent visitors at the Seaside Café and the little cottage by the bay. It would become our anniversary getaway. We looked forward to our stay and for the bowl of clam chowder. On one of our visits, we met Libby and her new husband Jackson. We floated the idea that if they ever decided to sell the seaside cottage we'd like to be notified. Libby just shook her head. I didn't blame her a bit. I wouldn't turn loose of it either.

ABOUT THE AUTHOR

Debbie lives in northern California with her husband and two rescue dachshunds, Dash and Briar. She avidly supports animal rescue and happily donates a percentage of book sales to local shelters and rescue organizations.

If you would like to find out more about Debbie and her books, visit https://www.authordebbiewhite.com

ALSO BY DEBBIE WHITE

Billionaire's Dilemma

Coaching the Sub

Christmas Romance – Short Stories

Made in the USA
Columbia, SC
27 March 2025

55757616R00083